Mme. Wadjinksi's
MAGIC
MIRR⬤R

JANET PATTERSON

Grosvenor House
Publishing Limited

This book is published by
Grosvenor House Publishing Ltd
Link House
140 The Broadway, Tolworth, Surrey, KT6 7HT.
www.grosvenorhousepublishing.co.uk

A CIP record for this book
is available from the British Library

ISBN 978-1-78623-916-7

LIST OF CONTENTS

MME. WADJINSKI'S
MAGIC MIRROR

North London, April 2012

It was a Monday morning, one of those mild spring days when white clouds scud across the sky, only to be replaced by dark threatening cumulus casting grey shadows across the ground beneath.

Kate was on her way into town to buy some sausages for her dinner, when she passed the antique shop on the corner. Although she walked past it almost every day, she had never been inside. Glancing casually in the window, she received a shock. For a few seconds she thought she saw a younger version of herself looking back at her. She stopped in her tracks and found herself looking at her own reflection in a mirror. It was bronzed with age, and through the glass front of the shop window it was hard to see clearly, but her image was indeed much more youthful. She retraced her steps and went in through the front door.

A bell tinkled as she entered the Aladdin's cave. A swarthy woman with an orange and yellow scarf round her head and large gold ear-rings dangling from her ear lobes was discussing the contents of a large crate with a blond haired youth in a black T-shirt. She must be

Russian, or Eastern European, thought Kate. Perhaps she was from one of those new-fangled countries – Serbia or Croatia or Slovenia or Slovakia – she got them all muddled up. Of course they weren't really new countries, just old ones with new names. Things had changed a lot since her schooldays. Kate was probably the only English person left on her street ...

'May I help you?' the Bohemian woman asked Kate, looking up from the box.

Her face was lined with deep crevices – probably the result of too much exposure to the sun, thought Kate. But her black eyes were bright and her face wrinkled into a broad smile, as if she wasn't aware of her own age.

'No, thank you. I'm just browsing,' replied Kate.

'Well, if you see anything that interests you, just let me know.'

The smile on her gypsy face seemed to linger.

Kate was so glad that the woman hadn't asked, 'How may I help you?'

That would have put her right off.

She went over to the mirror and looked at it more closely. Even at this distance, the patina seemed to blur her wrinkles and cast a soft rosy glow over her reflection. Her hair, cut just below her ears, was no longer grey and brittle, but stood away from her neck in soft honey-blonde waves. It was if the lines on her face had been air-brushed away. The flowery cotton dress that she had put on in response to the warm spring weather made her look tall and slender, rather than just thin and scraggy. A woman of her age spent as little time as possible looking in a mirror, but there was something charming and elegant about this one. It was oval-shaped and full length. The wooden frame was intricately carved and painted over with gilt, some of which had been chipped off. The Bohemian woman's reflection appeared behind her in the glass, peering over her shoulder.

'It is a beautiful mirror, isn't it?'

'Yes, it is, but I doubt if I could afford it.'

Kate always wore well-tailored clothes made out of good material, so that she often gave the impression of being better off than she really was. But in truth her clothes were well worn and slightly out of date. She hadn't been able to afford anything new for the past couple of years.

'It's French you know, Louis XIV.'

Kate laughed.

'Then I definitely can't afford it!'

'No, no, you mistake me. It's in the style of Louis XIV.'

Now it was the dark-skinned woman's turn to laugh.

'If it were an original, I would be a rich woman!'

Kate reached out to look at the price tag. As she had suspected, it was beyond her meagre budget.

'Don't worry about that!' exclaimed the woman. 'It's a special mirror for a special person. I will give you a good price.'

After jabbing at a calculator, she wrote an amount on a note pad. It was about 10% off the original price.

'I'll have to think about it,' Kate replied.

'Here is my number. If you decide to buy it, give me a call.'

The exotic woman handed Kate a card.

'Do you live nearby?'

'In Hollybush Crescent,' said Kate, tucking the card into her purse.

'In that case I can deliver it to you!'

'Thank you, you are most kind.'

Kate picked her way through the obstacle course of old furniture and paintings blocking her exit.

When she got outside into the fresh air, she took another glance at her reflection as she passed by the mirror. It definitely made her look younger she thought, as she continued on her way to the centre of town.

She returned home, replete with sausages.

That afternoon she couldn't stop thinking about the mirror. It was absurd. She didn't really need it, although she no longer owned a full-length mirror since she left her built-in mirrored wardrobes in Hampstead in an effort to downsize. It would prevent her from making the fashion error that many older women made of wearing something too long, or worse still, too short. The hem had to be just right. Of course, there were times when her bag didn't match her shoes, but when you are over 70, people are more forgiving. They probably think things like, 'Poor old dear, it's a wonder she can even get out of bed!' And it was a beautiful piece of craftsmanship. But it was too expensive. She really couldn't afford it.

She pulled out the card from her handbag. On a dark red background in gold lettering were the words:

> **Old Gold Antiques**
>
> **Mme. Wadjinski**
> **Purveyor of the Past**
>
> **638 7421**

Picking up the phone, she dialled the number.

The mirror arrived within the hour. The young man she had seen in the shop carried it upstairs, and Mme. Wadjinski came with him. He placed it in the corner of the bedroom and looked at it, sighing with satisfaction.

'Thank you, Erik. I'll see you tomorrow morning.'

As Mme. Wadjinski dismissed him, he tipped the cap that he wasn't wearing. Kate fumbled for her purse and gave him a couple of coins.

'He probably has more money than I do,' she thought to herself.

She got out her cheque book and started to fill in the details. Mme. Wadjinski took the cheque from her, glanced at it briefly, folded it and put it in her bag.

'I knew you were the person for this mirror as soon as you walked into the shop,' said Mme. Wadjinski.

'What do you mean?' asked Kate.

She had already purchased it. There was no need for further sales talk.

'It's a very special mirror.'

'What's so special about it?'

Mme. Wadjinski ran her bony fingers over the gilt frame.

'It will take you back in time!'

'What do you mean?' asked Kate, beginning to doubt her ears.

'Do you really want to know?' asked Mme. Wadjinski.

With a mischievous smile, she stepped behind the mirror. To Kate's amazement, she could still see Mme. Wadjinski through the mirror as if it were made of clear glass.

At that moment the room was infused by a reddish glow from the setting sun.

Kate stood gazing at the mirror, speechless.

Mme. Wadjinski beckoned her.

'Come! Think! There must be a time in the past you would like to return to?'

Without realizing how ridiculous her request sounded, Kate blurted out, 'Could I see my son again?'

'Of course, you can see anyone you like – your son, your husband, your mother ... But be warned – once you enter the Mirror World you will not be able to return!'

What did Kate have to lose? She was in her 70s, her beloved son was dead, her husband was living with a woman called Mary, and she was estranged from her daughter and two grandchildren. As Mme. Wadjinski reached out her claw-like hand, she took it and stepped through the frame.

Hampstead – 1982

Kate woke up with a start. She must have dozed off. What a strange dream! The mirror was in the corner of the room, but Mme. Wadjinski was nowhere in sight. But wait a minute! The room had changed, although it was all so strangely familiar. She looked around. The morning sun shone through the Georgian-style windows, casting a sheen on the silver and white striped wallpaper. She was back in her house in Hampstead, where she had raised her two children.

She was lying on the bed, fully dressed. Slowly she pulled herself into a sitting position. All her aches and pains had gone! She went over to the mirror and looked at her reflection. A woman in her early 40s, dressed in a black tailored skirt and a grey silk blouse, stared back at her. Her honey blonde hair had a few grey streaks in it, but her complexion was much smoother, with only hairline cracks etching out the harbingers of age.

She went downstairs to the kitchen and put on the kettle. Through the window she could see a neatly mown lawn surrounded by daffodils bobbing their heads in the spring breeze. She looked at the wall calendar – it was April 1982. Her son was still alive! She had drawn a red circle round 15th and had written something in ink. She had to squint to read her own writing – *Jason on leave!* But what was the date today? Had she missed his precious visit? How could she find out without running out into the street and asking someone?

Kate looked in her address book. It was full of names that were familiar but mostly forgotten. Some of them she hadn't spoken to in decades. She called Jill. It was strange hearing her voice after all these years, but Kate tried to stay calm and 'normal.'

'Oh, hello, Jill, how are you? Fine thanks. Listen, I have a silly question to ask. What's the date today, only I have a hair appointment and I can't remember if it's Tuesday or Wednesday, and I'd hate to miss it.'

'It's Tuesday the 15th? Oh, thanks. Yes, I'm fine. Sorry, I just got confused.'

'Yes, he is. That's probably why I can't think straight. Thanks a lot. 'Bye!'

She put down the phone, her hand shaking.

'It's today! He's coming home today!'

She patted her hair and smoothed down her skirt. Going over to the fridge, she opened the door to check on food supplies. It was fully stocked.

The front door slammed.

'Hello, Mum!' a cheery voice called out from the hallway.

Before she could collect her thoughts, the door opened and her tall, long-limbed son, handsome in his sailor's uniform, stood framed in the doorway.

She threw her arms around him and buried her face in his chest. She clung to him, her body racked with sobs. He put his arms around her and hugged her, kissing the top of her head.

'Jason! You're back!' she gasped.

'Steady on, Mum, you'll shrink my shirt!'

He pulled her gently away from him and seated her on a white kitchen chair, but her tears of joy were unquenchable. Embarrassed by her display of emotion, he pulled out a handkerchief and gave it to her.

She wiped her eyes and sat sniffing and gasping.

'Is the kettle on? I'd love a cup of tea!'

Kate stood up and turned to the counter, clattering around with the tea things in an attempt to pull herself together.

'So where's Dad?'

'Oh, he's away on business. You know what he's like, always working!'

'And Sandra and the boys?'

'They're fine – still up in Scotland. To be honest, I don't see them very often. They live so far away.'

'And how are you?' he asked, turning to her and taking both her hands in his.

'I'm fine. I'm just so happy to see you … How is the Navy treating you?'

'It's great. They're shipping me off to the Falklands in three days … '

At this, Kate started crying again.

'It's all right Mum. I've got to go, haven't I, otherwise they'll court martial me! Anyway, it will be good to see some action.'

She clung to him again.

'Please don't go! I beg you, please don't go!'

'Don't be silly. It's my job. Anyway, I want you to be proud of me.'

'I am proud of you, son. More than you'll ever know. Just tell me it's a war worth fighting.'

'Of course it is.' He repeated the words of his superior officer: 'The Argentinean president decided to reclaim the Falklands because there is an upcoming election, but it's a U.K. Overseas Territory, and entitled to our protection.'

She gave him a mug of tea, her hand shaking. Then she sipped at her own cup like an obedient child.

'What's for dinner?' he asked, opening the fridge door.

Hampstead – 1980

Kate was woken up by the sound of someone snoring. It was still dark. Then she realized – her husband was lying in bed next to her! She remained stock still for a few minutes, trying to assess the situation. Was this pre-Mary or post-Mary? She decided to test the waters by rolling over and snuggling up against him. He grunted and moved away.

She lay there wide-awake, a thousand thoughts swirling in her brain. When the alarm went off, she nearly jumped out of her skin. Howard got out of bed without switching on the light and went into the bathroom.

Kate could hear the swish of the water coming out of the shower. When he had to go to work early, he usually made his own breakfast, which would consist of a couple of pieces of toast and a cup of tea.

She got out of bed and put on a frilly dressing gown. Even though she couldn't see her reflection clearly in the dim light, she brushed her hair. Then she went downstairs and started to cook breakfast.

By the time Howard came downstairs dressed for work, eggs and bacon were sizzling in the frying pan.

'What's this in aid of?' he remarked, still grumpy from sleep. 'Is it my birthday?'

He tucked into the plateful of food while Kate nibbled at a slice of buttered toast.

'Will you be home late tonight?'

She didn't know why she asked. She thought she already knew the answer.

Howard stopped chewing and looked up at her, his light blue eyes round with astonishment.

'I thought Sandra was coming home today?'

'Yes, yes, of course. How silly of me!'

To hide her embarrassment and confusion, she stood up and examined the wall calendar. It was July 1980. One of the days was circled with a felt-tipped pen. She had written '*Sandra home from College.*'

'How could you forget?' he asked, looking at her as if she were demented.

'I didn't forget. I'm still half asleep, I suppose,' she stuttered.

'Of course I'll be home in time to see my daughter!'

'I'm sorry, I didn't mean to …'

Her voice trailed off.

Howard finished his breakfast and stood up, putting on his jacket. He came over towards Kate and gave her an absent-minded peck on the cheek. Then he picked up his briefcase and left. She winced as she heard the front door slam.

She sat there drinking her tea, trying to pull herself together. So Sandra was coming home! That would be nice. What would she cook her for dinner? She went over to the fridge and opened the door.

Sandra arrived about 3 in the afternoon. She dumped a bulging suitcase in the hallway and came into the living room. She was wearing a loose flowery blouse over jeans. Her brown hair, which she usually wore at shoulder length, was streaked with pink.

'Hello, darling, how are you?' Kate cried, jumping up to give her daughter a welcome hug.

Sandra hugged her back.

'I'm fine, Mummy. How are you?'

'Let me look at you! You've put on weight, and your hair ...'

Sandra pulled away.

'Oh, don't start, Mummy!'

'I'm not starting. It's just that every time you come home, you've done something different with your hair!'

'That's what you get for sending your daughter to Art College!'

Sandra flopped down on the sofa.

'Is there anything to eat? I'm famished.'

'Well, I can make you a sandwich. Daddy will be home for dinner at 6.30.'

Sandra followed Kate into the kitchen, where she prepared a snack. When she had finished, she sat down opposite her daughter and watched her eating.

'Are you all right, dear. You look a little pale. You haven't been staying up drinking to all hours, have you? I know what you students are like.'

'No, I'm fine,' Sandra replied, stuffing another gherkin into her mouth.

She swallowed and wiped the crumbs from her face.

'Mummy, I've got something to tell you.'

Sandra paused before dropping the bombshell.

'I'm pregnant!' she announced, then carried on eating.

Kate nearly spilled her tea on her lap.

'You're pregnant?' she repeated, the colour draining out of her face.

'Yes, I'm pregnant. I'm expecting a baby!'

'I know what pregnant means! When did this happen? I mean, how far gone are you?'

'Ten weeks.' Then she continued in a belligerent tone, 'I'm not getting rid of it, if that's what you're thinking!'

'I wasn't about to suggest such a thing!' replied Kate, even more shocked.

'Who's the father? I assume it's that boyfriend of yours from college ... what's his name?'

'Stuart. His name is Stuart.'

'How are you going to manage? With money I mean. We can't support you!'

'He'll find a job. We'll manage somehow.'

'You'll have to leave College. After all the money your father has spent on your education! You've ruined your career. You've ruined your life. You've ruined everything!'

Sandra sat silently while her mother ruminated over the situation.

'Is he at least going to marry you?'

'No, we don't believe in marriage. What difference does a piece of paper make?'

Kate stood up, outraged, making a clatter with her chair.

'That piece of paper is a legally binding contract.'

Her face was flushed and she was trembling.

'Marriage is founded upon a sacred oath, sworn before God!'

'So what happened with you and Daddy?' Sandra drawled.

At this point, Kate struggled with the urge to reach over and slap her face. She managed to control herself by holding on to the edge of the kitchen table. With tears of fury welling up in her eyes, she stalked out of the kitchen, and stormed up the stairs. She threw herself on her bed, where she lay crying.

A gentle hand touched her shoulder. She looked up to see Mme. Wadjinski. The surprise of seeing her there made Kate pause in her tears.

'What are you doing here? How did you get in?'

With a mysterious smile, she replied, 'I hold the key to all doors – past, present and future.'

Kate started to sniff again.

'There, there! Don't get upset!' Mme. Wadjinski cooed, handing her a tissue from the bedside table. 'Don't spoil the short time you have with you daughter with anger and tears!'

'But she's going to have a baby out of wedlock. My grandchild will be a … '

'Your grandchild will be an innocent baby. Listen, what's done is done. It's best to accept the situation. At least the father of the child will support his family – I know you don't like him.'

'He's such a drip ... and he's got a ring in his nose!'

'She will be able to lead him by it then, won't she?'

Kate gave a weak smile.

'Look, I know you don't like him, but he's her choice,' continued Mme. Wadjinski. 'Don't fight with her or you'll alienate her. You want to see your grand-child when he or she is born, don't you? Your daughter needs your support now more than ever.'

'I suppose you are right,' Kate blubbered.

'Go into the bathroom and splash your face with cold water. Then go down and talk to her.'

Kate did as Mme. Wadjinski suggested, but when she came out of the bathroom, her surprise visitor had disappeared.

London – 1961

'One more push! You're nearly there!'

She had been pushing all night, and now it was early morning. Her hair around her face hung in ringlets that dripped perspiration. Her face was red with exertion. She must look a sight! She hadn't slept properly for the past month because she had a belly the size of a camel's hump. And the pain! Whose idea was this anyway?

'I can see the head! The head is coming!' cried the nurse.

Suddenly, after all the effort, the head came out and the body just slipped after it. Kate sank back onto her pillow and closed her eyes. Then she heard a slap and a baby's cry.

'It's a boy!' the nurse exclaimed. 'You've just given birth to a beautiful baby boy!'

Kate opened her eyes again as the nurse brought her over a tiny red infant wrapped in a towel. A smile lit up her tired face. She had never seen such a dear little creature in her life – and he was hers!

'Can I hold him,' she asked, reaching out her arms.

'I'll just clean him up first, and then you can give him a feed.'

The nurse whisked him off as Kate closed her eyes again, utterly exhausted but feeling blissfully content.

A few moments later the nurse brought him back and placed him on her breast. Once he got the hang of it, he was feeding voraciously. Kate looked down at his tiny features; his fingers and toes were perfectly formed and his long eyelids curved slightly upwards at the end. The fluff on the top of his head was soft and dark.

After a few minutes, he fell asleep, a bubble of milk at the corner of his mouth and his hands still making clutching motions.

'I'll take him from you, shall I? Then you can have a rest.'

The nurse burped him and laid him in a cot next to her bed. Kate closed her eyes again and this time fell into a deep sleep.

She was at the bottom of a well and someone was calling her name. There was a circle of light at the top. As she floated up towards the rim, the voice got louder. She opened her eyes, and her husband was standing at the side of the bed with a foolish grin on his face and a bunch of red and white carnations in his hand.

'How are you dear?' asked Howard, bending over to kiss her on the forehead.

'I brought you these,' he added, placing the flowers on the bed.

'I'm fine – now. A bit tired. We have a son. He's over there.'

Kate indicated the cot with a slight movement of her hand on the bedcovers.

He went round to the other side of the bed and stood over the cot, clasping his hands together as if in prayer.

'You can pick him up if you like,' suggested Kate.

Cautiously Howard picked up the sleeping baby and tried to cradle him in the crook of his arm, but the child was so small and the man so big, that it took a few seconds for him to settle the infant comfortably. In the process, the baby woke up, struggled and began to cry.

'Don't drop him!' snapped Kate.

Antibes – 1959

Kate sat on the edge of the bed in her new pale blue satin and lace nightdress. Outside the open French windows she could hear the suck and crash of the Mediterranean.

There was a soft knock at the door.

'It must be the maid,' she thought.

She pulled on a matching negligee and opened the door a crack. It was Mme. Wadjinski!

'What are you doing here?' she gasped.

'I thought I would just come and see how you were getting on.'

'Come in!' she whispered. 'Sit down. My husband is in the bathroom.'

How strange those words sounded.

Mme. Wadjinski seated herself in an armchair. She looked the same as ever.

'So how are you? You look beautiful! How was your wedding?'

'It was wonderful. I'm fine – just a bit tired from all the excitement and the travelling.'

'And nervous?'

'A little,' she admitted, looking down shyly.

'Is this your first time, if you don't mind me asking?'

'Yes, it is,' she replied, blushing scarlet.

'Do you love him?'

'Yes, very much.'

'And does he love you?'

'Yes, he does.'

'So there's nothing to worry about,' she said, leaning forward and patting Kate's hand. 'Everything will be all right!'

A voice came from the bathroom.

'Is there someone else in there, dear?'

'It's only the maid,' she called back.

Kate turned towards the armchair, but it was empty. The curtains leading to the balcony billowed in the breeze.

1957 – Richmond

'Hurry up, Kathleen, he'll be here soon!' her mother called from downstairs.

Kathleen appeared at the top of the stairs wearing a crisp white shirt-waister with a stand-up collar, a wide red patent-leather belt that clinched in her slender waist, a full skirt boosted by thick petticoats, and red high-heeled sling-back sandals. Her golden blonde hair was swept up in a chignon.

Her father stood dumbstruck in the hall, watching her descend the stairs, her head held high like a model. She gave him a cool superior smile and passed into the kitchen, where her mother was preparing the tea things.

'You look lovely dear!' she said, handing her daughter a tray. 'Carry these into the dining room for me, please.'

The table was set with the best bone china. The silver and crystal sparkled in the afternoon sun slanting in through the open French windows.

Her father had followed her into the dining room and stood watching her with his hands behind his back as she placed the Victoria sponge cake next to the pile of cucumber sandwiches. The diamond ring on her left hand glittered in the sunlight.

'You will be nice to him, won't you Daddy?'

'I hardly know anything about him,' he replied, sucking his unlit pipe.

'Well, that's why he's coming, so that he can meet you both!'

'He might at least have asked me first before proposing to you,' her father grumbled.

'Well, he will ask you, only there's no sense in asking your permission before asking me, is there? Supposing I had said no?'

'Things were done differently in my day. I call it bad form!' he grunted.

'Well, I'm not giving the ring back!' retorted Kathleen.

Her mother had followed her into the dining room carrying a pot of home-made strawberry jam in a cut-glass jar and a plate of scones in the other. She sensed a storm brewing.

'What is it that he does for a living?' she asked.

'I've told you before, he's a salesman.'

'Trade!' sniffed her father.

'It's a perfectly respectable job. He earns good money, and he may soon become area manager!'

Her father sat down in disgust and started reading *The Times*.

'You will say yes, won't you, Daddy?'

Her father hunched up his shoulders and pretended to be absorbed in his newspaper.

'It's just that, well, we don't think he's good enough for you,' interjected her mother.

'No father ever thinks that any man is good enough for his daughter,' commented Kathleen.

'He's not even a Catholic!' complained her mother.

'Nobody cares about that sort of thing now. Mixed marriages are quite commonplace. Anyway, he says I can bring up our children any way I please.'

'And your career! You haven't finished at secretarial college yet. You're so young to throw it all away!'

At that point the doorbell rang, and everybody jumped. Kathleen lost her *sang froid* and went rushing off towards the hall.

'Open the door, dear!' called her mother as Kathleen hurried upstairs.

'No, you open the door!' she called from the top of the stairs. 'I want to make an entrance!'

In the end her father opened the front door. A tall handsome man in a suit stood holding a bunch of mixed flowers.

'You must be ... ' remarked her father.

'Good afternoon Mr. Harper. I'm Howard – Howard Nesbitt.'

He held out his hand to reveal a pair of gold cufflinks. Mr. Harper shook his hand reluctantly.

Howard's face lit up as he spied Mrs. Harper standing behind her husband. He smiled broadly to reveal a set of even white teeth.

'These are for you, Mrs. Harper,' he said, leaning forward with the flowers.

'Oh, thank you,' replied Mrs. Harper, blushing and smiling as she accepted them. She could see how her daughter might find his charm and good looks irresistible.

'Well, you'd better come in,' suggested Kathleen's father grudgingly.

As he stepped into the hall, Kathleen started her descent. Howard whistled in admiration.

'You look beautiful!' he exclaimed.

Richmond – 1945

Katie awoke to the trill of a blackbird sitting on a branch outside her window. She was in her old bedroom, where she had grown up.

Somewhere below a dog barked.

'It's Kim!' she cried, running downstairs and out into the back garden.

Kim was sitting in Katie's old playpen with her last remaining puppy. She jumped up and wagged her red tail when she heard Katie's voice. Katie leaned over the pen and threw her arms round Kim's neck.

'Oh, Kimmy, I love you so!'

Kim's mother was a red setter. Nobody knew what her father was. Every time Mummy said this, for some reason people would laugh.

Her mother came outside to pick some runner beans.

'Oh, Mummy, do we have to give Snowy away? Can't we keep him?' Katie pleaded.

'I'm afraid we must. I've promised him to Mr. Giles.'

'But supposing Kim dies? Please let me keep Snowy!'

'Don't be silly, dear, Kim isn't going to die. Whatever gave you that idea?'

Her mother went back into the house, carrying the beans in a colander.

Katie climbed over the rail and sat down in the pen with Snowy on her lap, while Kim stood in front of her, gazing at her with her brown eyes and wagging her tail.

Later that afternoon, while Katie was playing in the garden, the doorbell rang. Mr. Giles appeared at the back door. Katie had seen him before because he lived nearby. He had come to take Snowy away. She pleaded with her mother again, but she ignored her. As her mother handed Snowy over to Mr. Giles, Katie felt a terrible stabbing pain in her heart. She ran up to her room and sobbed into her pillow.

'Why are you crying, child?'

Katie stopped crying and looked up in surprise. Mme. Wadjinski was sitting on the end of her bed.

'Oh, Mme. Wadjinski, they have taken Snowy away, and Kim is going to die!'

'Listen, Katie, in Mirror Time, you only go backwards into the past. You cannot go forwards to the future. The future is past! So that when you wake up it will be yesterday, and Snowy will be here!'

'And Kim? Does that mean that Kim doesn't die?'

'That's right. She'll just get younger and younger, like you.'

Katie sat up and wiped her eyes. Mme. Wadjinski sat next to her.

'Let me explain something important. You have five years left to you, either in Real Time or Mirror Time. It doesn't make any difference. So you will spend the next five years here with Mummy and Daddy and Kim, and each day you will grow younger.'

'So will I be a baby again one day?'

'Yes, that's right, dear. A beautiful little baby.'

'And then what will happen?'

Mme. Wadjinski paused before answering.

'Well, in the end, you'll go back to where you came from.'

'You mean, I'll go back to God?'

'Yes, my child, you'll go back to God!'

IF DOGS RULED THE WORLD

(A One-Act Play for 2 Dogs and 1 Person)

An elegantly trimmed white poodle is sipping her *latte* at the breakfast table. She is wearing a red leather collar studded with diamantes.

The phone rings. It is her friend, Spot the Dalmatian.

Phoebe: The Poodle Residence. Phoebe speaking! ... Hello Spot! How are you?

Spot: Aarrrf aarrrf woof woof!

Phoebe: Listen, you'll never guess! I've got a new Person! I know, I said I would never have another one after Benjie died, but I saw him at the Rescue Centre, and he's so adorable, I just couldn't resist him.

Spot: Aarrrf aarrrf woof woof woof?

Phoebe: I'm sorry, what did you say? Does he have a pedigree? (Phoebe gives a tinkling laugh.) He's a mongrel – a young male, about 14 years old, with olive skin, brown curly hair and big blue eyes. He's looking at me now! He's so cute! Oh, wait a minute, I think he wants to go out. He keeps scratching at the door.

He's very well trained. When I take him out, he hangs on to the lead as if his life depended upon it. He doesn't realize that all he has to do is let go, and he would be free! Of course, I let him unhook it so that he can go behind a tree and do what he has to do, but he still holds on to it, even when it is no longer attached! I suppose it gives him a sense of security – I think he's terrified of returning to a life on the streets, living on scraps and sleeping rough on cold winter nights. He's got used to the regular meals and a comfortable bed.

And he's so playful! He loves throwing sticks! I have to keep retrieving them for him and it gets a little tiring after a while, but he seems to enjoy it.

But he's getting a bit too frisky, if you know what I mean. Last week we were walking along the promenade when I met Rover ...

Spot: Aarrrf woof woof?

Phoebe: You know Rover – the sheep dog with the ginger female. Well, we let them off their leads and in two flicks of a lamb's tail they were sitting together on the bench and nuzzling each other. In the end I had to nip Ginger's ankle – it was the only way I could separate them! I've booked an appointment at the doctor's for next week so that he can have his Operation … '

Spot: Woof! Woof! Woof! Woof! Woof!

Phoebe: I know, it does seem cruel. I hate to do it, but it's for his own good. You can't have hundreds of people milling all over the place with no dogs to take care of them.

Anyway, I'd better go – he's rattling the door handle and whimpering. I need to take him for a W-A-L-K. He's so intelligent – I swear he can understand every word I say! I'll meet you in the park in five minutes. Chow!

THE HOMECOMING

Romani stood in Kennedy Airport looking up at the revolving slats of the Departures Board, oblivious to the people pushing past him with their luggage carts. Gradually the destinations came to rest, and his heart leapt as the name of the town that he had been searching for appeared: Lapitzi!

'Home of my fathers,' thought Romani to himself. This was the moment he had longed for, when he would eventually return to Grozniczi, the land of his parents' birth.

He sat down with his backpack on a row of seats all joined to each other, lit a cigarette and looked around. A couple of stewardesses strutted smartly past him towards the gates, trailing their neat trolleys behind them like exotic birds with long tail feathers. Most of the people rushing past or seated near him were well-dressed, some wearing business suits. Others, apparently going on vacation, were dressed more casually. Romani had taken short trips within the U.S., but had never travelled beyond the borders on a long-haul flight, so he was dressed comfortably in jeans and a T-shirt.

The P.A. announcement echoed in his ears as he pushed his cart over the carpet towards the check-in desk. His luggage was bulky, as he had packed sweaters and other warm clothes and shoes in preparation for the cooler climate. Relieved of the heavy suitcase, he made his way through passport control and security.

The smell of expensive perfume tempted him into a duty-free shop. He wandered past the packaged bottles of whisky and other alcoholic drinks in a daze. Not wanting to buy anything too heavy or bulky, he ended up purchasing a large carton of cigarettes.

Walking past a fast food restaurant, he caught a whiff of hamburgers, but the smell only made him feel nauseous. His stomach was in a knot of anticipation.

When the announcement came for him to board his flight, he found his way to the waiting area, where he could hear the deadened roar of giant planes landing and taking off outside the window.

His heart was pounding as he boarded the plane, where he was greeted by a pretty air stewardess dressed in a red suit and a pillbox hat tilted to one side. She had the familiar high cheekbones and dark eyes that were characteristic of his people.

'Good morning, sir! Welcome to Grozniczi Airlines! Please pass along the gangway.'

He struggled down the narrow aisle and eventually found his seat. After he had settled down, he looked around the half-empty plane. All the instructions were in both English and Groznian, which made up for the drab interior.

The cabin crew stepped forward to demonstrate the safety equipment. They spoke in English and Groznian. Because his parents had spoken their native language in the home, he was able to understand what the airline staff were saying. Everything was strange yet familiar.

As the plane bounced down the runway, he clutched the arm rests, but shortly after take-off the plane reached its cruising height, and he began to relax and to think about his trip to Grozniczi.

What was he expecting from his visit? He really didn't know. His mother had often shown him the photograph album, and his father used to tell him about the adventures he had had growing up in the countryside as a boy, but of course everything had changed since the Russian invasion. Would he be able to find the orchards where his father went scrumping for apples, or the stream where he fished as a boy? Would anything be left of the house where his father grew up? Sadly, both his parents had passed away in 1992, just before Grozniczi had become a republic. Now seemed an opportune time for his visit, in memory of his parents and in celebration of his 40th birthday. He wondered if there had been much progress in the two years since Grozniczi had gained her independence.

He opened his wallet and pulled out a colour photograph that he always carried with him of his parents, taken about 10 years ago in their back yard. His father stood proudly by the vegetable patch, his arm around his mother. He was tall and gaunt with sallow skin, his body wasted by early years of want. His dark wavy hair was streaked with grey and his sad black eyes peeped out cautiously from under bushy eyebrows. Thin lips smiled from beneath a thick moustache.

Still wearing her apron, his mother, a small bony woman with wispy brown hair and prominent features, smiled back at him in the golden light of the afternoon sun.

He had left the rest of the photos behind for safe keeping in the family home in New Jersey.

Romani looked out of the window to his left, but all he could see were clouds, and beneath them the sea. He searched around for the headphones so that he could watch the movie, only to realize that there were none. Neither were there any screens.

'Ah well,' he thought, settling back in his seat, 'welcome to the Republic of Grozniczi!'

After what seemed like an interminable flight, punctuated by several disappointing meals and a touchdown in London to refuel, the plane began its final descent. It was much cloudier than the take-off, and after several lurches and stomach-churning drops, the wheels touched Groznian tarmac. He pulled his denim jacket out of his hand luggage and put it on over his T-shirt.

The flight attendants bade him goodbye, wishing him a pleasant stay, and he descended the gangway onto Groznian soil. Running parallel to the runway was what looked like a cluster of farm buildings. Romani made his way towards a cavernous shed marked 'ARRIVALS,' buttoning up his jacket against the blustery wind. The clouds were dark and lowering, gathered together as if to block out any ray of sunshine. He was glad he had thought to pack a thick sweater that his mother had knitted for him.

The Arrivals Lounge was a draughty old shed without adornment.

'They've turned the air conditioning up too high!' he thought to himself.

Then he realized that there was no air conditioning.

He waited by a rickety carousel to collect his luggage, which was easy to spot as his suitcase was by far the newest and most expensive of all the baggage that came off the plane. As he pulled it off the conveyor belt and headed through a tunnel towards the Immigration Shed, he began to feel the effects of tiredness and jet lag. He had been up since 3.30 a.m.

A dour, ill-shaven official in a crumpled jacket sat at a counter protected by a sheet of glass. Behind him lounged a police officer in a worn uniform, his arms folded, a gun at his hip. As the other passengers in front of him passed through one by one, Romani began to feel anxious. It suddenly occurred to him: his parents may still be on a black list for fleeing the country illegally. But surely the new government would welcome back people who had rejected the old regime? It slowly dawned on him that the people now in control had grown up during war and oppression. They would not remember how it was when his parents had played in the fields as children. They probably didn't even know the meaning of the word 'democracy.'

'Bojorni!' Romani grinned nervously, stuttering as he attempted to greet the immigration officer in Groznian.

The officer stuck his hand out through a gap in the window, ignoring Romani's attempt at friendliness.

'Paseporti!'

Romani handed over his shiny American passport. The officer held it up to his nose and sniffed at its newness. Then he flicked through the stiff pages. When he came to Romani's personal details, he muttered something to an assistant sitting at a desk. In front of him was a heavy, handwritten ledger. The clerk turned the pages laboriously while the officer examined the photograph. Now he turned his attention to Romani's face, his black piercing eyes scrutinizing him suspiciously. Not for the first time that day, Romani felt his stomach churning. The second hand of the clock on the wall of the Immigration Office jerked forward one tick at a time. The officer glared at his visa. Surely there could be nothing wrong with it? Romani had obtained it from the Groznian Consulate in New York. After several uncomfortable minutes, the clerk mumbled something, and the officer brought down his stamp onto the passport.

Romani found himself beaming with gratitude and relief as he passed on through customs and outside to the taxi rank, where a couple of battered cars, built in the '70s, were standing. The driver of the first car sat with a hand-rolled cigarette in his mouth. Romani held a piece of paper through the half-open window and indicated the name of the hotel. Without bothering to remove the cigarette, the driver grunted and nodded his assent. Realizing that the taxi driver had no intention of budging from his seat, Romani walked around to the trunk. He had no trouble opening it, as the lock was broken. He hauled in his smart suitcase and pulled down the door to the trunk that did not close properly.

❧❧❧

After a bumpy drive across flat, featureless countryside, they entered the town of Lapitzi. Having passed along wide half-empty streets lined with blocks of grey buildings, the taxi drew up outside the Grand Hotel on Stanislav Square. As he entered the lobby and looked up at the dingy chandeliers and the threadbare treads on the dark red carpet that lined the sweeping marble staircase, the phrase 'faded elegance' sprang to mind. The elevator was not working so he followed the porter up the stairs, running his hand along the chipped balustrade. The porter unlocked the door to his room and stood there waiting for a tip. Romani threw his backpack on the single bed and reached into his pocket to pull out a few coins, which the porter stared at before dropping them into the breast pocket of his unironed shirt. He grumbled something that Romani didn't quite catch by way of leave-taking.

The first thing that Romani noticed about the room was the musty, damp smell and the darkness. He tried to pull back the discoloured velvet curtains, but the cord was broken. He had to push them back manually, releasing faint puffs of dust as he did so.

He looked down onto the square below him through unwashed windows. In the middle stood a bronze statue of a man on a horse covered in verdigris and bird droppings. He couldn't see who it was, but it was leaning at a precarious angle, as if someone had tried to pull it down. There were dents in the surface, and the pigeons had commandeered it as a convenient perching place. The square was lined by buildings, some old and damaged, with pock marked stonework and the tell-tale soot trails of fire. Others were modern office blocks and apartment buildings, abandoned in the process of being built. Some of the shops were boarded up. Dwarfed by a windowless high-rise stood a crumbling church, grey with pollution, its onion-shaped spire decorated with swirling mosaics, the only bright feature in an otherwise bleak landscape.

It had started to rain.

Romani washed his hands and splashed his face at the cracked sink. The tap was tarnished and there was no plug. The cleaner had failed to remove a long black hair. He walked across the worn linoleum and sat down on the narrow bed, removing his sneakers and dropping them onto the grubby mat. Lighting a cigarette, he lay back on the flat pillow and exhaled smoke through his pursed lips. Opposite him on the wall, hanging at a slight angle from the picture rail, was a photograph speckled with fly dirt of a frowning man with a moustache, dressed in a military uniform.

'Well, at least it isn't Stalin!' he thought to himself.

When he had finished the cigarette, he stubbed it out in an ashtray that had not been emptied since the previous guest had used it. His stomach had settled down from the flight, and he was beginning to feel hungry.

Getting up off the bed, he opened his suitcase and pulled out a knitted sweater, which he put on under his jacket. Downstairs in the lobby, the receptionist directed him to a bar further along the road that served food.

It was easy to find as it was on the same block. He opened the door and walked in. A handsome, big-boned man with thick dark bristling hair stood behind the counter. His off-white shirt was rumpled and there was stubble on his chin. Apart from the barman, the room was empty.

'Do you serve food?' Romani asked tentatively.

'Food? Food? Yes, we serve food. Sit down!' roared the barman, indicating one of several empty tables.

Then he shouted at a door at the back of the bar.

'Marí!'

A tall waitress appeared in what Romani recognized as national dress – a low-cut broderie anglaise blouse, with a laced-up bodice and an embroidered woollen skirt. Her brown curly hair fell around her neck and shoulders. She had attractive features, with pronounced cheekbones and eyes that slanted up slightly at the ends, but she wore no make-up and her expression was stony.

'What you want?' she asked.

He had not been offered a menu.

Recalling a lentil stew with dumplings that his mother used to make, he asked, 'Do you have szlotzi?'

'Szlotzi? Szlotzi!' The waitress grew indignant. 'No szlotzi! Hamburger or hot dog?'

'Errrrr, hamburger please. And do you have French fries?'

She looked at him.

'Patatis,' he said, making a chopping motion.

'Ah, patatis!' She almost smiled. 'And to drink?'

He tried to remember the name of the national beverage, but it escaped him.

'Coca Cola, please.'

She disappeared through the door behind the bar. Romani sat in silence, listening to the muffled sounds in the adjacent room. At that moment the front door crashed open. Three men in belted tunics, baggy pants tucked into leather boots, wearing their peeked caps at various angles, came in and sat down at a table in the far corner. The barman brought them a bottle of vodka and then came over with his Coke.

'Ruski!' he muttered, and spat at the sawdust, just missing the toe of Romani's right foot. 'Filthy pigs!'

Eventually, Marí appeared with the hamburger. A handful of sad, soggy French fries sat beside it. He called out to the barman, but his voice was drowned by the three Russians, who were getting louder and more boisterous by the bottle.

After two more attempts he attracted the owner's attention.

'What you want?'

'Do you have any ketchup?' he asked, making a shaking motion with his hand.

'Ketchup? Ketchup?' The barman treated his request with contempt. 'Where you think you are? America?'

The hamburger and bun were dry and the lettuce was wilted. He was almost grateful for the flat, lukewarm Coke that he drank to wash it down.

Romani pushed his plate back feeling far from satisfied, and looked around at the establishment. It must have been very elegant in its heyday, with art nouveau designs etched on the smoky mirrors and hand-painted tiles halfway up the wall. Now it looked dingy and uncared for, with paint flaking off the upper part, and the wooden floor worn and splintered.

He took out a pack of Marlboro's and lit a cigarette. The barman picked up a bottle and two glasses and made his way over to the table. Romani looked up at him, pleasantly surprised. Perhaps the owner was feeling a need to socialize, and had chosen him for want of more suitable company. The bear-like man grunted as he pointed towards the empty chair.

'Please, sit down!' invited Romani.

The man placed his large bulk on the small cane chair and looked at him with his world-weary eyes, saying nothing. Romani held out the pack of cigarettes and the barman took one, lighting it with a match. He sat back, inhaling deeply, and blew a stream of smoke towards the ceiling. His face wrinkled into a satisfied smile. He filled the two small glasses with a dark liquid from the sticky bottle.

'Here, Coca Cola boy. Try a man's drink!' he cackled, pushing one glass towards Romani.

The barman raised his glass.

'Proszt!' he called out, before downing it in one.

Remembering the Groznian toast, Romani followed suit. The liquid was strong and sweet, a bit like cough mixture, though not unpleasant. After a few seconds, he felt a warm glow inside.

'We don't get many foreign tourists in Lapitzi,' the barman remarked.

The comment stung.

'My parents are from here – well, not from here exactly, but from Grozniczi. They fled to America in 1954.'

The barman drew on his cigarette. His next words came out in a cloud of smoke.

'So, they ran away!'

For the second time, Romani smarted from his words.

Then the barman sighed heavily, gazing down into the cherry-coloured liquid in the glass before him.

'Still, I don't blame them. It was probably for the best.'

During the pause that followed, Romani became aware of the Russians singing and banging the bottle of vodka, now empty, on their table. Reluctantly the barman pulled himself up and strolled over to them. As he picked up the empty bottle, one of the Russians made a comment that Romani didn't understand. The publican moved towards the bar like a saddle-sore cowboy, picked up a full bottle of vodka, unscrewed the top and placed it deliberately on the table. He returned to Romani's table, the lines deepening between his eyes.

While the barman sat in a morose silence, Romani took the opportunity to ask for directions.

'So can you tell me how to get to Mroz?'

'Where?'

The barman turned round and shouted at the door behind the bar.

'Marí! Bring the map!'

A few minutes later, Marí appeared with an old map that was disintegrating at the folds. Romani hoped that Mroz wasn't located too close to a crease.

They moved their glasses to one side as Marí placed the map on the table. She scanned it, muttering the name of the village to herself.

'Is it near a larger town?' she asked.

'My parents sometimes spoke of Ludz.'

'Ludz,' she muttered. 'Ah! Here it is! And there's Mroz!'

Both men pored over the map, staring at the end of her tapering fingernail.

'Can I get a train to Ludz?' asked Romani.

'Train!' the barman scoffed.

He stood up.

'Come,' he beckoned, his voice softening.

Romani followed him over to the window, where the barman placed one hand on Romani's shoulder and pointed with the other.

'You see the far corner of the square, where that fluorescent sign says *Hotel*? You can catch a bus there at 10 o'clock tomorrow morning. It stops at all the big towns going East. It's your best bet.'

Romani thanked his hosts and bade them farewell, leaving the half-full pack of Marlboro's on the table. The rain was now falling in a steady downpour. Although it was only a short sprint to the Grand Hotel, the rain soaked through his jacket to his woollen sweater.

As he slid between the cold sheets of his single bed, he asked himself, 'What am I doing here?'

❧❧❧

The next morning the rain had cleared up; puffy white clouds hung in a blue sky. Romani was at the bus stop long before 10 o'clock, afraid of missing the coach and having to spend another dreary night in Lapitzi. The bus arrived 20 minutes late. He followed the other passengers on board and was relieved by the driver's assurance that it stopped in Ludz. He sat down on a wooden seat next to a woman wrapped in a shawl, clutching a bundle on her lap, and looked around. He could hardly see out of the grimy windows. There were cigarette ends and other garbage on the floor. The stench of stale smoke and unwashed bodies pervaded the bus.

Soon they were out of Lapitzi and bumping along the road through more rural areas. They travelled through farmland speckled with cows and sheep, pine forests, past lakes and through mountains. While the scenery was picturesque, fresh and green from the rain, many of the villages had a sad, deserted feel. Every now and again the bus rolled past crumbling stone buildings, lacerated with shrapnel. Even after all this time, there were still scars from the Russian occupation.

It started to rain again, and continued to do so, on and off, for the next few hours. An old woman sitting across from him had shared some bread stuffed with an indeterminate filling. He was grateful for her kindness and hospitality.

He was even more grateful when Ludz came into view.

Above the tiled roofs, the globe-like dome of the church gleamed gold against the silver sky. The approach to the town lay through fields on either side of the road. Some were cultivated, others had been left fallow. They passed a farmer sitting huddled on a plough drawn by a pair of oxen, which plodded along the furrows, straining under a double yoke. Rusting farm implements lay scattered about the fields. There were no modern tractors or other motor-driven vehicles to be seen.

Soon the bus was driving past rows of wooden houses on the outskirts of the town. They all had small gardens at the front, some carefully tended with flowers and vegetables, others abandoned and overgrown with weeds. Most of the houses needed a new coat of paint, the original colour on the weatherboarding having long since faded. Some were in a state of disrepair, their shutters hanging off their hinges to reveal gaping black holes where window frames had once been. Now and again they would pass a gap between two houses, where grass and wildflowers had grown over the remains of a burnt-down building.

Romani climbed down the steps, his body aching from the long drive, and took a deep breath of fresh air. It was still raining.

His fellow passengers had dispersed, some on foot and others in the horse-drawn carriages waiting by the bus stop. Only a horse and cart remained. A scowling figure, dressed in a black overcoat gathered at the waist with a leather belt, his unkempt hair sticking out from under a peasant's cap, stood hunched next to his bony nag.

Romani approached the driver.

'Can you take me to Mroz?' he asked.

The man shook his head morosely.

'It's 12 miles away, then I have to come back.'

'I'll give you 30 roubles.'

His moustache drooped and he sighed.

'I do it for 100!'

'Fifty roubles then.'

The driver gave a shrug of resignation and indicated with a jerk of his thumb that Romani should get in the back. There was a tarpaulin on the floor, which he pulled over himself in an attempt to keep dry. The rain was now falling heavily. The driver gave a shout and a crack of the whip as the cart lurched forward, juddering over the potholes in the muddy road. The wind picked up and the rain pattered down on the tarpaulin. Now and then they would pass a house reduced to rubble.

'Why you go to Mroz?' called the driver over his right shoulder, a note of indignation in his voice. 'There's nothing there. The Ruskis destroyed everything – the houses. They burnt the fields. They did bad things to the women. Many people fled.'

'My family is from there.'

'Perhaps you find them in the graveyard.'

Romani shuddered and fell silent.

On the brow of a hill, silhouetted against the stormy sky, the driver passed a row of burnt-out skeletal structures dripping with rain. They reminded Romani of gallows.

The mare picked up her pace as they descended the slope and entered a spinney, a carpet of red and yellow leaves creating a slippery path under the horse's hooves. The filigree branches of the near-naked trees stretched up towards the grey sky.

By the time they emerged from the wood, the rain had stopped.

Romani found himself looking down upon a valley surrounded by fields, and in the middle, a small village, not much larger than a hamlet. At that moment, the sun broke through the clouds.

'Mroz!' the driver announced contemptuously.

As they entered the main street, the driver turned round, 'So, did you book a hotel?'

His sarcasm was not lost on Romani.

'I'm looking for Castle Street, Utilizi Schlossi.'

The driver didn't understand his pronunciation. Romani leaned forward and showed him the precious piece of paper he had been guarding in his breast pocket.

An old man loped by with a skinny dog.

'Senori! Utilizi Schlossi?'

The old man looked at him in bewilderment, and for a moment Romani was afraid it no longer existed.

'What?' he asked, cupping his hand to his ear.

The driver repeated the question and the old man nodded his head slowly.

'Ya, Ya!'

Then he began waving his arms about as he gave directions.

Shortly afterwards, they arrived at one end of the street.

'I can't see any castles!' the driver sneered.

'This is fine, thanks.'

Romani paid the driver, who looked at the bank notes as if they had been contaminated by nuclear waste, and stuffed them in his waistcoat pocket.

He got down. The driver turned the horse and cart round and shouted back over his shoulder, 'Good luck!'

Romani started walking along the unpaved road, dragging his suitcase behind him. The houses were built of stone, some of which had been destroyed. A goat hopped lightly over the rubble to reach a tuft of grass growing out of a remaining wall. Further down an old woman sat crouched on her stoop, smoking a pipe. She was dressed in black, but wore a brightly coloured woven shawl. As he drew nearer, she pulled the pipe out of her mouth and stared at him, her mouth open, transfixed. Fearing he had alarmed her by his appearance, he stopped in his tracks. The old woman pulled herself up, visibly shaken, leaning on the doorjamb for support. A husky sound emitted from her throat. At first he couldn't understand what she was saying, but as she repeated the word, it became clearer and shriller.

'Josefi! Josefi! Josefi!'

Her gnarled hands reached out to him.

He stared at her in disbelief, his mouth gaping open.

'No, I'm not Josefi!' He could hardly speak for the choke in his voice. 'He's my father! I'm his son, Romani!'

But she didn't seem to understand.

'Josefi! You have come back! My son!'

She clasped him in her bony arms and, sobbing with joy, pressed her face against his chest.

Romani held the frail old woman to him, his eyes filling with unexpected tears.

As her gasping sobs eventually subsided, she released him and pulled a crumpled red spotted handkerchief from her skirt pocket, dabbing at her eyes. Now she was grinning all across her wizened face, revealing a few remaining teeth that were stained and crooked like tombstones.

'Come! Come!' she gestured, gazing up at his face with her bright black eyes.

She pulled him into the house by his sleeve.

They entered straight into the kitchen and living area – 'open plan' as it would be called in America. An appetizing smell wafted from a pot of stew simmering on the stove that was fuelled by firewood. A loaf of freshly baked bread stood on a cooling rack next to the sink. The walls in the kitchen area were blackened by soot.

In the middle of the living room stood a battered wooden table covered with a hand-embroidered cloth. The rest of the furniture was old and worn. Squinting in the dim light, Romani could make out a row of silver-framed photographs that were lined up on a shelf at the back.

The old woman lifted her head and shouted, 'Tomasi! Come and see who is here!'

There was some shuffling and banging overhead, then a pair of boots appeared at the top of the stairs, followed by long legs clad in worn jeans. Then came a hand-knitted sweater, and last of all a weather-beaten face crowned by a head of black wavy hair, greying at the temples.

Romani and Tomasi stood looking at each other in bemused astonishment. Tomasi was about the same height as him, thinner but sinewy. His face was swarthier, but apart from these details, Romani could have been looking at an image of himself in five years' time.

'Tomasi! It's Josefi!'

Romani stepped up to him and held out his hand. 'I'm Romani, Josefi's son.'

'I'm Tomasi, Sonja's son,' he replied, clasping his hand in a firm grip.

'So we must be … '

'Cousins!' exclaimed Tomasi, throwing his arms around him and clutching him in a bear hug.

When they eventually pulled away, Tomasi sniffed and wiped the moisture from his eyes.

'Come, Josefi. Sit down!' his grandmother called. 'You must be hungry!'

She ladled some stew into a bowl and placed it in front of him along with a thick slice of brown bread. He looked up at her beaming face, her eyes still shining with tears.

'Szlotzi?' he asked.

'Ya, ya, szlotzi!' she replied, patting him on the shoulder.

THE CURSE

The clatter of typewriters and the flicker and buzz of a faulty fluorescent light were irritating Jane to screaming point. She forced herself to carry on working, in spite of the thumping headache and the sickness in her stomach, but it was no good. In the end she went in to ask her boss if she could go home early, before the headache developed into a full-blown migraine. She could tell he was annoyed. He made some comment about 'another one of your headaches.' She felt guilty because there was a pile of work to do, but she had no choice.

Clutching her beige handbag and her raincoat, she entered the dimly lit lift that shuddered its way down to the car park. She crossed to where her Renault stood waiting. The smell of petrol was making her feel nauseous. Her head spinning, she drove out of the covered area into the centre of town. She had forgotten it was market day. Even though it was early afternoon, the streets were still congested. Every traffic light seemed to be against her. The screech of brakes and the honking horns made her feel worse. The headache was pulsing in her temples now, and she could hardly wait to get home and lie down in a darkened room.

With a feeling of relief she reached the leafy suburbs and arrived at Acacia Avenue. After passing rows of semi-detached houses with well kept front gardens, she eventually turned into her driveway and parked the car in the garage, alongside her husband's Ford Fiesta.

'What's he doing home so early?' she wondered.

She could hear Bruce howling in the back garden. As she opened the gate, a gangly Irish wolfhound stood up in his kennel and let out a series of sharp staccato barks, at the same time rattling the chain around his neck. It was more than she could bear.

'Hush, Bruce, lie down!' she snapped.

With a whimper he slumped onto the floor of his kennel, resting his chin on his folded front paws and looking up at her with resentment in his eyes.

But why was he chained up? He was usually given free range of the back garden. Tim only restrained him when they had visitors who did not like dogs.

'I'll deal with it later,' she thought to herself.

As she let herself into the kitchen by the back door, she almost slipped on a half-eaten banana on the linoleum. She picked it up and threw it in the bin.

'That's strange!' she thought to herself.

Tim was usually the neat one. It was as if someone had eaten it in a hurry and had just thrown it down.

That was when she heard a moan and a thumping sound coming from upstairs. She froze, feeling sick to her stomach. What was going on? She had never thought of her husband as the type to play around, but then, you never knew. By now her head was pounding and she couldn't think straight. What was she walking into? Tim with another woman? It was unthinkable! Or another man? Worse still! She slipped off her low-heeled shoes, quietly opened the door leading into the hall, and crept up the carpeted stairs in her stockinged feet.

When she reached the landing she noticed a strange musky smell. It reminded her of a zoo. The bedroom door was ajar, and the noise had stopped. She could detect the sound of breathing. The mirrored wardrobe door was open, so that she could only see the reflection of her own white face and dark ringed eyes, round with fear. She glanced over at the bed, which was still made up with a rose-pink satin quilted eiderdown, as she had left it that morning. Then another thought occurred to her. Perhaps her husband was trying on her clothes! Horrible as the idea was, at least it would be easier to handle than the other alternatives. Her heart was pounding and her mouth dry as she stepped forward and swung the mirrored door shut with her fingertips. Then she screamed and her vision went black all around the edges as she fell into a faint.

Her husband's voice called her back into consciousness: 'It's all right dear, it's only me.'

Reassured, she opened her eyes, and screamed again. She was looking up the nostrils of a gorilla! She pulled herself up, hanging onto the bedcovers, and backed towards the door.

The gorilla put out an arm towards her and spoke: 'There's no need to be alarmed, dear, it's me, Tim!'

By now she was leaning against the doorpost, gasping for breath, clutching her blouse at the throat.

'Come and sit down on the bed. Let me explain.'

It really was Tim's voice.

She perched on the edge of the bed.

'Mrs. Dawson down the road put a curse on me!' expounded the talking gorilla.

'Mrs. Dawson put a curse on you?' Jane whispered faintly.

'About six months ago I was out walking Bruce when he slipped his lead. He ended up chasing her cat, and she cursed me.'

The gorilla shrugged his huge shoulders helplessly.

'Can the curse be removed?' asked Jane, now full of concern. 'You should see a doctor!'

The gorilla laughed self-deprecatingly.

'A doctor won't be able to help. It's gradually wearing off. It used to last for about two hours every afternoon. Now it's down to one and a half. I've been taking time off work. I wanted to tell you, but I knew you would be shocked.'

'Well that explains the brown hairs I found under the bed!' replied Jane. 'I thought you were having an affair!'

They both laughed.

At that moment, the church bell struck four.

The gorilla started.

'It's the hour of my metamorphosis. Go downstairs. You won't want to watch this!'

Jane didn't move.

'No, we'll go through this together!'

First the hair started to fall off. Then he let out a blood-curdling scream as he writhed and twisted on the carpet. His whole body lost mass, and his features became distorted into a horrible grimace before her eyes. After a few agonizing minutes, her husband stood before her, thin, pale and bald. Jane sat on the bed, petrified, all trace or thought of a migraine forgotten.

Tim recovered more quickly than she did.

'I know it's all a bit of a shock, love. Why don't you lie down and I'll make you a nice cup of tea.'

Jane stretched out obediently on the bed, as he pulled the eiderdown over her.

He went downstairs and within a few minutes she could hear the kettle whistling. She just lay there, staring at the ceiling, not knowing what to make of it all. You think you know someone after 23 years of marriage and then you come home to find your husband has turned into a gorilla!

He brought a tea tray upstairs and, after helping her to sit up with the aid of a pillow, placed it across her lap.

'Thank you, dear, I needed that,' she said, sipping demurely from the china cup.

Tim sat down beside her and held her hand, patting it gently with the other. When she had finished, she put down the cup and smiled weakly.

'I quite liked you with a hairy chest!' she commented.

The next day, Jane informed her disgruntled boss that she would be working mornings only in future. She wanted to be with Tim during his darkest hour.

And so she hurried home every afternoon to stay by her husband while he went through his grotesque transformation. After a few months, the power of the curse became weaker, until it wore off completely. Bit by bit, life returned to normal along Acacia Avenue.

One winter evening, Jane and Tim were sitting across from one another warming their feet in front of the electric fire. Jane was knitting a Fair Isle jumper and Tim was reading his newspaper.

With a sigh, Jane paused in her knitting and lowered it onto her lap. A dreamy smile crossed her face as she looked up at her husband.

'You know, Tim, I quite miss the way you used to be – you know, when you were a simian.'

'I could always buy a gorilla suit,' he suggested, with a twinkle in his eye.

THE MAN IN
THE SOUP KITCHEN

Sunday

May loved working in the soup kitchen. She lived by herself, so she usually cooked small portions. But in the soup kitchen, everything was on a large scale. Most of all she loved the cheese grater. She would feed in chunk after chunk, press the button, and the cheese would come out in a big pile, all nicely grated.

Sometimes the volunteers were short of helpers and they had to work extra hard and fast, but there was always a feeling of satisfaction after they had finished serving and were clearing up the dishes.

The food was prepared in the basement of a church on Sunday mornings, so she was not able to attend the service, but she always remembered a picture of praying hands from childhood that said, 'Hands that serve are holier than lips that pray.'

Although most of the men were grateful for the free meal, there were a few who swore at the servers or made obscene suggestions. However, May made allowances for them because it was hard living on the streets, and many of them were drug addicts or alcoholics.

She had noticed one man in particular who came in every week. Even though his hair was unkempt and his jacket was dirty and rumpled from sleeping rough, she could tell he was a cut above the others. His sweaters were made of cashmere, and he was always softly spoken and polite. He looked a bit like Richard Gere, which didn't hurt.

Sometimes he hung around after he had finished his coffee. But many of them did. It was bitterly cold in the winter, and most of the men had nowhere else to go. May wondered how they survived the sub-zero temperatures. Of course, some of them didn't.

Luke always looked for her on the serving line. She had long wavy strawberry blonde hair and a soft sweet face. She was definitely not from around here. New York women had a sharp edge to them. She must be from the Mid-West. She always gave him a big smile and looked straight at him with her eyes as blue as a summer sky. She called him 'Sir,' which gave him back a fraction of his self-esteem. But of course, she called everyone 'Sir.' Still, he appreciated it.

Monday

'Did you have a good weekend, then?' asked the manager of the bookstore in the West Village where May worked.

'Yes, thanks!' she replied.

'So, did you do anything interesting?'

Carla always asked the same questions. What business was it of hers what May did in her free time?

'Not really. Worked in the soup kitchen.'

'You really have to get out more!' quipped Carla. 'What are you doing? Looking for Mr. Right?'

Wednesday

It was another night of biting cold. May's long woolen coat flapped open to expose her knees above leather boots. She pulled her hat down over her ears and sank her neck into her collar. The snowflakes stuck to her eyelashes and almost blinded her as she made her way towards the brownstone building where she lived on East 10th Street. Her heart contracted as she noticed a strange man huddled in the outer lobby. At first she was nervous. He might have a knife or try to take her bag. But he was probably some poor homeless person sheltering from the wind and snow. She took her key out beforehand, so that she wouldn't have to stand and rummage in her bag.

As she opened the first door, he nodded to her and mumbled, 'Hi!'

She gave a tight-lipped grimace and nodded back. Then she looked at him more closely. Her faced relaxed into a smile.

'Don't I know you? You're the man from the soup kitchen!'

'I'm just trying to keep warm,' he explained, as if an excuse was necessary.

'You must be freezing!'

She hesitated for a heartbeat while she fumbled with the key in the lock.

'Would you like a cup of coffee?'

'I'd love a cup of coffee!'

As she let him into the warm inner lobby, her head was spinning. What was she doing, inviting a strange man into her apartment? She had read so many stories in the newspapers ... Still, he seemed like a decent guy.

'It's much warmer in here!' he remarked, smiling and rubbing his hands together as they entered the elevator. May pressed the button to the third floor.

She unlocked her front door and led the way into her apartment. They entered through the kitchen, which opened into the living room. It would never make it into *House Beautiful*, thought Luke, but it was one of the coziest, most welcoming apartments he had ever seen. The walls were covered in framed posters and the furnishings were bright and cheerful – it reminded him of the '60s.

'This is a lovely place,' smiled Luke, looking round approvingly.

'Thank you! Have a seat! Oh, let me take your coat. It must be wet.'

He took off his coat and handed it to her. As she put it on a hanger in the bathroom she couldn't help noticing that it was well-cut despite its shabbiness.

'What would you like?' asked May. 'Coffee? I've only got instant. Or would you prefer tea? I've got black, green, herbal, Lapsang Souchong ...'

'Coffee will be fine thanks.'

'Light? Black? With sugar?'

'Regular with no sugar.'

She spilled a handful of cookies onto a plate while the kettle was boiling.

'So, how long have you lived here?' asked Luke, still looking around as if he were in a fairy palace.

May motioned towards the settee.

'Eight years, so I don't pay much rent. I was lucky. I found this place before they started gentrifying the area. The landlord would love to get me out.'

She placed the coffee and cookies before him on a side table next to the couch. Luke wanted to gobble them down, but managed to pace himself. Soon there were only crumbs left.

'So, how long have you been living on the streets, if you don't mind me asking. My name's May, by the way.'

He leaned forward and shook her hand.

'Luke, Luke Andersen. A month. It's been the hardest four weeks of my life! Just when you think your life can't get any worse, then this happens!'

'Where were you living before?'

'I rented a studio in the Wall Street area, close to where I worked.'

He was aware of May's face, shining with curiosity.

'I used to be an investment banker!' he added.

'You're kidding!'

'I know – I've come down in the world – from Wall Street to skid row!'

'What happened? Did you lose your job?'

'I was married and living in Long Island with my wife and daughter. We started fighting – I guess she got tired of me working late. So I moved out and we got divorced. I started drinking, and ended up getting fired.'

'Didn't you have savings – or investments?'

'I had some money of course, but I had to pay the mortgage on the house, alimony and child support. The payments were assessed on my earnings at the time. Soon my money ran out, and I couldn't even afford the rent on the studio.

'Couldn't you apply for another job?'

'It's hard to go on an interview when you haven't had a shower and your clothes are dirty. I did some gardening work on Long Island for a while, but it didn't pay enough.'

May looked down and noticed the empty plate.

'Oh, you must be starving! Listen, I was going to cook dinner for myself – it's only spaghetti bolognaise – would you like some?'

'It's the best offer I've had all day!'

May put on *Dire Straits* and busied herself in the kitchen. She said something about the weather in an attempt to make conversation but he didn't answer. She looked over towards the couch. He had fallen asleep.

When dinner was ready May placed the dishes on the table, making as much noise as possible in the hope of waking him up. She called his name a couple of times but by this time he was snoring. Going over to him, she shook him gently by the shoulder. He woke up with a startled look on his face, raising his arm in a defensive gesture.

'Oh, I'm sorry, I didn't mean to frighten you. Just that dinner is ready.'

May indicated the table with the food set out. He came and sat down. Even though she had given him a hearty serving of pasta, he still finished before she did. She then offered him some carrot cake that she had made herself.

'This is great! Thanks a bunch. You're a good cook!' He wiped the crumbs from his face and fingers. 'I haven't eaten like this for a long time.'

After the meal she cleared away the dishes and he relaxed again on the sofa. May continued her interrogation.

'So where do you sleep?'

'Sometimes I stay in shelters but they are not safe. Some of the men carry weapons and they'll rob you if you are not careful. Usually I sleep in doorways or on the Subway.'

'What do you do about taking a shower or washing your clothes?'

'Some of the shelters have showers.' He motioned to a filthy back pack. 'I carry a change of clothes, but they are dirty at the moment. I usually go to a launderette.'

'Well, you can wash your clothes here if you like. There's a washer and drier in the basement. Would you like me to wash them for you?'

'Yes, but there won't be time for them to dry properly.'

They exchanged glances.

'You can come by tomorrow to pick them up!' suggested May.

Luke pulled his dirty clothes out of the bag and gave them to her.

'Does it matter if I wash them all together?' she asked.

She took them down to the basement and dropped them into the machine. When she returned to the apartment, he had fallen asleep on the couch again. She washed the dishes as quietly as possible, trying not to disturb him. Then she went down and transferred the wet clothes to the heat drier.

Luke was still sleeping soundly. She looked out of the window. The snow was falling thick and fast outside. The street was deserted, except for a couple of cars driving slowly through the slush. She didn't have the heart to wake him up and turn him out into the cold night. She fetched a blanket from her bedroom and covered him with it. Before going to bed, she went down to the basement one more time to bring up the warm, slightly damp laundry and hung it on a rack in the bathroom.

It was still early, so she sat in bed and read, but she was unable to concentrate on the book. She couldn't stop thinking about the stranger asleep on her couch.

She must be crazy! She could never tell her mother what she had done! She didn't even have a lock on her bedroom door. Still, he seemed like a nice man, just down on his luck.

May turned out the light and tried to sleep, but she tossed and turned, feeling a mixture of excitement and apprehension.

Her alarm went off at 6.45 a.m. It made her start and she felt groggy from a lack of restful sleep. Then she remembered Luke. She put on her dressing gown and opened the door carefully. He was still curled up on the sofa, sleeping like a baby. She tiptoed into the bathroom and took a shower, emerging with her damp hair wrapped in a towel. Ten minutes later, she came out of the bedroom, dressed for work. After putting on the kettle,she started to prepare breakfast. The whistle finally aroused Luke. For a few moments he looked surprised and confused, but when he remembered where he was, a smile crossed his face.

'Hi! Did you have a good sleep?' asked May, standing in the kitchen area shoveling Wheaties into her mouth.

'Yes thanks, the best I've had for a long time.'

'I'm just making some coffee. Would you like some?'

She took him over a cup of coffee.

'I have to rush off to work, but just help yourself to breakfast. You can have a shower if you like. Just close the door behind you when you leave.'

'Thanks for everything, May. You've been so kind. I don't know how I can repay you.'

May set off for work with a spring in her step. She realized that she might come home to find her valuables missing and the place trashed. People did strange things. But the truth was, she didn't have many valuables. She bought things that she liked, rather than expensive items with designer labels to impress other people. And you had to take a risk sometimes.

May was a cheerful person by nature, but Carla noticed that she was in exceptionally good spirits.

'You're very chipper today! What happened? Did you find yourself a boyfriend?'

'Maybe!' she replied, smiling mysteriously to herself.

'Don't tell me! You met someone at the soup kitchen!'

May leant forward over a delivery of books to hide her pink cheeks.

Carla's remark had stung her. But then, available men were few and far between. Everyone knew that good-looking men in New York were either married or gay. And he had been successful at one time. He was just going through a bad patch.

࿐

That evening May hurried home from work. She wasn't sure what she would find.

She looked up at the window but to her disappointment the light was out.

She turned the key in the door and pushed it open cautiously. There was still a faint odour from his clothes,

59

but the place was empty. Luke had left it more or less tidy. The blanket was folded and there were some washed dishes on the draining board.

She opened the bathroom door. His clean clothes were still there.

The door bell rang. He must have been waiting across the street, watching for the light to go on.

'Who is it?' May asked through the intercom in a trembling voice.

'It's me, Luke, I've come to collect my clothes.'

She buzzed him in.

She stood holding the door open, listening to the whirr of the elevator as it clanked up to the third floor. Luke stepped out and turned towards her, his face lighting up. He was still wearing his dirty clothes, but he must have washed his hair and had a shave. He really did scrub up nicely.

May felt like greeting him with a hug, like an old friend, but just in time she remembered that she hardly knew him. She invited him in and offered him a cup of coffee, which he accepted.

'Thank you for letting me stay here last night. I feel like a different person!'

As she packed her groceries away, she asked if he would like to stay to dinner.

He stood, looking down at the floor. She could tell that he was dying to say yes, but felt embarrassed.

'Listen, I can't go on living off you like this.'

He shrugged helplessly, turning up his hands.

'But if I turn you out on the streets, what will happen to you? You'll never get out of your situation and it will just be a downward spiral for you.'

❧❦❧

He finished off his dessert with a satisfied sigh. May leaned forward, placing her elbows on the table.

'Listen, I've been thinking. Why don't you apply for a proper job?'

He opened his mouth to reply, but she pressed on.

'I could type up your c.v. at work. All you need are decent clothes. You must still have some.'

'They're in boxes in the garage on Long Island. Even if I could collect them, I would have nowhere to put them.'

'I've got a brother who has a van. He could drive us out at the weekend and we could pick them up. You could leave them here.'

Luke looked embarrassed.

'I don't want to see my wife. She has another boyfriend now.'

'When was the last time you saw your little girl?'

He answered with a catch in his voice, 'Nearly two years.'

Looking down he added, 'I'm too ashamed to face her.'

'But she must miss you! It would be selfish to avoid her. Anyway, think about it.'

She started clearing away the dirty dishes.

Before she left the next morning she lent him 50 dollars so that he could get his hair cut and buy a few other things that he needed.

'I can't take money from you!' he protested.

'You can pay me back later.'

Saturday

It was a joy to be driving along with the ocean sparkling to the right. The snow on Long Island was pristine, covering the winter landscape with a thick layer of dazzling white. So different from the snow in Manhattan, which had a grubby, second-hand look.

'Here it is!' called out Luke, pointing to what looked like a mansion, silhouetted white against the deep blue sky. A long curving driveway swept up to a flight of steps, flanked by colonnades. On either side of the porch, wide bay windows reflected the snow-covered lawns and the green-blue sea. Clumps of snow weighed down the branches of bushes and trees. Now and again a white blob would slide off a branch which would spring back, relieved of its burden.

'Wow!' commented May's brother.

'Is this your house?' asked May, incredulous.

'Not any more,' came the bitter reply.

'Shall I turn into the driveway?' asked Bob.

'No!' Luke replied. 'I can't bear to face my wife.'

'We can drive up to the garage door, and then Bob and I can ring the doorbell,' suggested May.

A tall elegant woman wearing a red tailored trouser suit with sequins on the lapels opened the door, cigarette in hand. She looked May up and down briefly. It didn't take her long to make her appraisal.

'Hi, Mrs. Andersen. My name's May and this is Bob. We've come to pick up Luke's things,'

Then she scrutinized Bob, as if trying to figure out his position in the triangle.

'They're in the garage,' she said, indicating the building where the van was already parked with her hand, which still held the cigarette.

'Thanks,' replied May. 'We won't be long!'

'You're welcome. I need the space.'

A gruff voice came from behind her. 'Who's that, Sue Ellen?'

'Nobody, just some people to pick up Luke's things.'

At that moment, a little girl's head appeared from behind her mother.

'Who is it, Mommy? Is it Daddy?'

Then the child spotted Luke by the van, squeezed past her mother and ran towards him, shouting, 'Daddy! Daddy!'

He scooped her up in his arms and hugged her. She clung to him like a koala bear.

Bob and May walked over to the garage and started loading up the van with suitcases containing Luke's clothes. Luke put his daughter down gently and came towards them, wiping his eyes on his sleeve.

'Do you need anything else?' asked May.

He pointed to a couple of boxes marked *Shoes*.

After they had finished, May and Bob got into the van while Luke said goodbye to his daughter.

By now she was sobbing and clinging to his legs.

'Don't go, Daddy! Please don't go!'

He gently disentwined himself.

'I must, darling, but I'll come back and see you again.'

'When, Daddy, when?'

'I'll come back real soon, honey, I promise.'

He got back into the van and waved to her as they pulled out of the drive, her wan, tear-stained face turned up towards him, shining white in the reflected light of the snow.

Luke was quiet on the drive back to Manhattan. Bob helped to carry the boxes and cases into May's apartment, after which he kissed her on the cheek and said goodbye to her.

'Won't you stay, at least for a cup of coffee?' asked May.

'No thanks, I've got to go to work this afternoon.'

After Bob left, May went into her bedroom and started to take her summer clothes off their hangers and pack them in boxes. Then Luke hung his suits next to her winter clothes. She also put her sandals in a plastic bag to make room for Luke's shoes on the floor of the wardrobe. She hid her boxed up clothes behind the sofa and covered them with a purple Indian bedspread.

'There, that wasn't so difficult, was it?'

May looked across at his forlorn face, and her heart went out to him.

'I'm sorry, I meant the packing. It must have been hard for you going back.'

He shrugged.

'Never mind, you'll be able to go back and see your little girl again.'

'You don't know my wife. She'll try to stop me!'

'But why? You have visiting rights, don't you?'

'Yes, but I'm behind on alimony payments and child support. She has threatened to sue me. I think her new boyfriend is behind it!'

'How much do you owe, if you don't mind me asking?'

'About $7,000.'

May thought of her little nest egg, sitting in her savings account, waiting for a rainy day.

'Look, I've got some savings ... '

'I wouldn't dream of taking your money, May. You've already done more than enough for me!'

'Well, we'll think of something. Couldn't your wife move to a smaller house?'

'She doesn't want to. She says that Amie is happy at her school, and doesn't want to move.'

After lunch, Luke drafted his résumé.

'This is impressive! We'll get you back on your feet in no time!' exclaimed May as she glanced over it.

That night, Luke slept on the sofa as usual. May had a restless night, thinking of the day's events, and of the money she had in her bank. She got up to get herself a drink of water. As the fridge clicked open, she heard Luke cough. Perhaps the light from the fridge had woken him up.

'I'm sorry, Luke. Did I disturb you?'

'No, I couldn't sleep.'

'Would you like a glass of water?'

May filled a glass from the tap and took it over to him, sitting down at the foot of the sofa to watch him drink. He thought she looked like an angel in her long white satin nightdress with her hair spread out over her shoulders, shining like spun gold in the street lights. She took his hand and squeezed it softly.

'Don't worry. Everything will be all right. We'll find a way.'

As she released his hand, it rested on her knee. He started to stroke the silky material of her nightdress.

'It has been such a long time since I caressed a woman,' he thought.

Then he reached up and pulled her down towards him. She did not resist.

That was the last night he spent on the couch.

Sunday

The next morning, May decided to give the soup kitchen a miss. Instead, they went out for breakfast to B & H on 2nd Avenue. It was a tiny restaurant that served home-made Kosher dairy food, and was famous for the excellence of its cuisine, the cheapness of its menu and for the owner, who routinely showered his customers with verbal abuse. Fortunately he liked May, and Luke looked so distinguished in his clean clothes that they were spared the humiliation. Another young woman was not so lucky. She asked for a glass of water in a nasal, reedy voice. The owner mimicked her.

'Oh, so you want a glass of waader?'

To her embarrassment, he kept repeating it. The other customers started to smile. Then someone sniggered. In the end, everyone laughed out loud, including the victim of his ridicule.

Luke and May sat smiling at each other, holding hands under the table while they waited for their French toast to arrive.

Afterwards they picked up *The Sunday Times*, which resembled a small tree trunk in weight and size. Usually May stood at the cash desk of the supermarket and sorted through the sections, throwing away anything she wasn't interested in – the Sports Section, the Business Section, Real Estate, to make the paper lighter and easier to handle, but this time she left it intact. Luke tucked it under his arm and carried it with ease. When they got home, Luke started looking through the Employment pages and marking off anything he found of interest.

Monday

During her lunch hour the following day, May sat at her computer and typed up Luke's résumé, along with several letters of application. Carla passed behind her.

'Aren't you going out to lunch? You should get some fresh air.'

'No, thanks, I'll pick up a sandwich later. I just want to write some personal letters, if that's O.K.'

Carla peeped over her shoulder. There was nothing May could do to stop her.

'What are you doing? Applying for another job?'

Two Weeks Later

Luke received a couple of rejections to his applications. Then one evening May came home to see him grinning all over his face. He could hardly wait for her to get inside the door.

'I've been for an interview with a stock market firm on Wall Street!'

'How did it go?' asked May, placing her groceries on the counter and unwinding her scarf from her neck.

'I think it went well. The only problem was explaining what I had been doing for the last couple of years.'

'So what did you tell him?'

'I told him the truth. He said he admired my courage and determination.'

One month later

Luke loved his new job, although he often came home late and exhausted. At first May understood his need to establish himself and do well, but after a while, she began to sympathize with his ex-wife. Still, he regained his confidence by the day. He gave her back the 50 dollars she had lent him with his first week's pay. Soon he started to repay the loan, bit by bit. May was happy for him, but sometimes she thought back to the first few weeks and remembered how happy they were at the beginning.

Luke was usually too tired to hold a proper conversation in the evenings. If May chatted away about her day at work or asked too many questions, he would become irritable and snap at her.

In the morning he would get up early, and leave before she had taken a shower.

They would still go out at weekends, but the tension between them during the week began to take its toll.

Six months later

One evening Luke was exceptionally quiet at dinner.

'Is there something the matter, Luke? You've hardly spoken a word all evening.'

He looked up at her.

'I've found another apartment.'

May felt a strange feeling in the pit of her stomach. What did he mean? Had he found a larger place for both of them, or did he want to move out?

'I thought you might like your space back,' he explained.

May did not like the direction this was going.

'I don't want my space back. I want to be with you!'

'We can still be friends. You can come and visit!'

There was a moment of silence while May absorbed what he was saying.

'Is there someone else?'

'No, of course not!'

'You've met someone else, haven't you?'

'No, I swear …'

'What's her name?'

'Candy.'

May felt as if someone had just punched her in the stomach.

'Candy? Candy! What kind of a name is that?' demanded May, repeating the name in a nasal, mincing voice.

'It's short for Candice ... '

'Oh, it's short for Candice. And where did you meet Candice?'

'At work.'

'What is she, your secretary?'

May's voice rose in pitch.

'She's a colleague – a stock broker ... '

'Oh, so she's a stock broker with a hooker's name!'

'Stop it, May! It doesn't become you.'

'Oh, it doesn't become me, does it not?' She was almost shrieking by now. 'So tell me, what does become me?'

Before he had a chance to answer she went on.

'I took you in off the streets, I put you back on your feet, and this is how you repay me! After all I've done for you! What am I? A ... a ... doormat?'

She stood up abruptly, shoving back the chair, and stormed into the bedroom. Pulling all his clothes out of the wardrobe, she threw them in a heap on the living room floor. Then she tossed out his shoes, one by one. They landed with a clunk.

'You can take your suits and your designer shirts and ... and ... '

As May stood before the pile of clothes, the reality of the situation hit home. She sank down on the edge of the bed and hid her face in her hands. Then her shoulders started to shake as she burst into tears.

Luke stood speechless, not knowing what to say.

'What has she got that I haven't got?' she gasped between sobs. 'What can she give you that I can't? I've given you everything!'

Luke sighed wearily.

'Perhaps that's the point. She admires me. She sees me as a winner. You will always remember me as a loser. To you, I will always be the man you met in a soup kitchen.'

THE HUNTED

He rose with the sun, while the dew was still wet upon the grass. As he stepped outside the cottage, the autumn chill in the air caused him to shiver. On the far side of the courtyard, a chestnut horse awaited him, pawing the ground beneath the birch trees that flickered yellow and gold. The stallion nuzzled his master in greeting as the man placed a saddle upon his back. The hunter leaped up and swung his leg over the horse in one agile movement and sped off towards the woodlands, his wavy brown hair streaming behind him like the wind.

First he checked his snares one by one, only to find all of them empty.

'How curious,' he thought. 'Perhaps there have been wolves in the forest.'

But there were no signs of fresh blood on any of the traps.

Then he saw her in a clearing. A fallow deer, all on her own, not much bigger than a fawn. An easy target, he thought, as he reached back, pulled an arrow from his quiver and positioned it nimbly in his bow. But she had disappeared. He crossed the clearing into the woods. There she was, standing behind a tree. He laughed to himself. Did she think she was hiding from him? Again he drew back the string of his bow, but she was gone. He mounted his steed and followed her on horseback, but the crackle of dead leaves and twigs under Umballa's hooves betrayed his presence. Every time he thought he had lost her, he saw a bright eye looking at him through the foliage. He loosed several arrows, but to no avail.

The undergrowth grew thicker, encumbering his progress, so he dismounted and, after tethering Umballa to a tree, pursued his quarry on foot. The forest became denser. He took his knife from his leather belt and hacked at the brambles that were barring his way. His progress was slow, yet still she kept appearing and disappearing. Was she playing a game with him?

As the morning wore on, he became obsessed with slaughtering his prey, but the more arrows he loosed, the more she evaded him. His frustration was making him tired and thirsty. He paused to drink from a leather flask, strapped across his leopard-skin jerkin. He wiped the back of his hand across his mouth and forehead. Even though the air was still frosty, perspiration poured down the hunter's face.

The chase continued until the sun was above his head. Eventually he came out into another clearing, surrounded by copper beeches, at the foot of a mountain. The deer was standing at the mouth of a cave. Now he had her! In a frenzy, he shot off two more arrows as she disappeared behind the rocks. Reaching back into his quiver, he realized that he only had one left. Still, she was trapped. It would be easy to corner her. He followed her into the cave.

The entrance opened out into an enormous cavern. He stood for a few moments blinking, adjusting his eyes to the gloom after the bright daylight. It was like a huge, dark cathedral, smelling of damp earth. Filled with a sense of awe, he lifted his eyes, but he could not discern the upper reaches of the cave. Only the faint flap of bats, disturbed in their midday sleep, told him of its height.

At the far end, the hunter spotted the white flick of the deer's tail in the dim light as she turned into the entrance of a tunnel. He heard an ominous rumble and a roar behind him as he took off in pursuit of her. Stopping in his tracks, he turned around to see rocks falling over the mouth of the cave. The thunder of the avalanche shook the ground beneath his feet like an earthquake, and filled his heart with terror. He had no time to retreat. Besides, it was too dangerous. He could be struck by one of the tumbling boulders. The avalanche had cut off his escape route. Now he was trapped! The only way was forward.

Blinded by darkness, his heart thudding in his breast, he followed the curve of the tunnel, holding on to the wall with his right hand. As the crash of the last boulder died down, he became aware of the deer's hooves tapping on the rocky floor. The tunnel twisted and turned. It was pitch black. He could hear the drip of water. Gradually it became lighter. He must be at the other side of the mountain! The tunnel finally brightened and widened into a second cave. The deer was standing at the entrance, looking back at him, silhouetted by the light. As he reached for his last arrow, she turned and frisked away.

The hunter followed her to the entrance, where he came to a halt. Before him, stretched out beneath his feet, lay a land of rolling hills and wooded valleys. The sky was a deep blue, the air warm and balmy.

To his left a cataract roared. The glittering water cascaded down over the rocks from the snowy mountain top, gathering in a blue-green pool, where it eddied and gushed down the slope to a stream at the bottom of the hill. Even from a distance he could see salmon leaping in the sunlight.

On the other side of the stream lay a golden meadow surrounded on three sides by a wood, but there was something strange about it. Some of the trees were adorned with pink and white blossoms! Perhaps he had reached the legendary Land of Eternal Spring that he had heard the old men talk of in the taverns. Until this moment, he had dismissed it as a fairy tale.

In the far distance on the horizon stood a line of dark green pine trees pointing like arrows against a cornflower blue sky.

A sparrow hawk cried above his head. Instinctively, the hunter reached back for his last arrow, only to remember that he was saving it for the deer.

He had been so bewitched by the magical land that he had almost forgotten about her. She must have escaped by now.

Shielding his eyes from the sun with his hand, he surveyed the landscape. Just in time he caught sight of the deer's hindquarters disappearing into the wood. He descended the rocky slope and forded the stream that gurgled over the boulders. The clear cold water came up to his knees.

As he crossed the meadow, the sweet scent of wildflowers wafted on the gentle breeze. Bees buzzed and butterflies danced over blood red poppies and white meadowsweet.

Upon entering the shady wood, he looked around for any trace of his prey. The long grass was pushed down where she had trodden. Following her tracks, he continued in pursuit. The trees grew denser, and at times he thought he was lost, but then she would appear again, always remaining beyond his arrow's range.

Finally the hunter emerged from the forest. He stopped in his tracks and gasped in astonishment at the sight before him.

Below him lay a large circular clearing, surrounded by all manner of beasts and fowl, like Noah's Ark: foxes and chickens, wolves and rabbits, vultures, horses, snakes and monkeys, all sat peaceably together in a semi-circle, predator next to prey. Many he had seen before, some he had only heard of. A leopard and panther sat like statues side by side in the middle of the horseshoe. At the far end, on a rock, stood a magnificent white stag. The deer approached the stag, bent her front legs and touched her head to the ground.

The stag opened his mouth, and, to the hunter's amazement, a booming voice issued forth from his throat:

'Well done, Sister Deer. You have risked your life to bring us the Hunter! Brother Man, step forward!'

What strange land was this where animals could talk?

The hunter turned around to see if he could escape, only to shrink in fear at the sight of the black panther sitting directly behind him. The panther's muscles rippled under his black shiny coat. His green eyes glinted at him and he opened his mouth to reveal a pair of fangs dripping with saliva. The hunter was staring into the jaws of death. For the first time in his life, he felt helpless with fear. His hand went to his knife, but he realized that it would be a useless defence against this powerful beast.

'Touch your head to the ground!' growled the panther.

The hunter crouched and bent forward as he was bidden.

The white hart's voice bellowed again.

'Brother Man, lay down your weapons!'

The hunter placed his bow and arrow, knife and dagger on the ground before him.

'You have arrived at the Court of the Wild Kingdom, brought here at my request by Sister Deer. Let us proceed. You are accused of the wanton killing of our brothers and sisters! How do you plead?'

The hunter's heart was pounding wildly as he spoke with a shaky voice. It occurred to him that perhaps he was on trial for his life.

'It is true that I hunt and kill animals, but it is my living! I have a wife and children to provide for.'

'I am told you kill in excess of your need, and that you do it with bloodlust.'

The stag turned to the assembled animals.

'Who will speak against this man?'

A squirrel limped to the centre of the circle.

'Speak, Sister Squirrel!'

'Your Honour, I was caught in this man's trap. There was much blood and I screamed in pain. I struggled all night to no avail. At daybreak I managed to escape with my life, but I lost my foot.'

At this point, she held up a stump.

A gasp shattered the stillness.

'Thank you Sister Squirrel. You fought bravely for your life. Who else will speak?'

A young fox, barely larger than a cub, stepped forward.

'Speak, Brother Fox!'

'Your Honour, this man killed my mother when I was but a cub, leaving me and my two sisters to fend for ourselves. My dear sisters died of starvation.'

'The fox killed the chickens!' protested the hunter.

At this, a gaggle of hens sitting near the front erupted into cackles.

'One at a time, please!' commanded the stag. 'I can't hear what you're saying!'

A plump black bantam waddled forward.

'Sister Hen!'

'Henrietta, your Honour.'

'Henrietta, please speak!'

Fluffing up her feathers, she turned and pointed a wing towards the hunter.

'HE killed the chickens! He stole them from the farmer's wife, who depended upon them for eggs!'

'Thank you, Henrietta. You are brave to tell the truth.'

Then the leopard stood up and walked to the centre of the circle. A silence descended upon the arena.

The stag spoke in gentle tones: 'Sister Leopard – Princess, speak!'

She hung her head and said in a choked whisper, 'This man killed my beloved mate and stole his fur. Now he wears it upon his back!'

All eyes turned to the hunter.

'Give her back the coat!' commanded the stag.

The hunter started to remove the jerkin, but he hesitated at the thought of the chill that would descend with the setting sun.

'Give her back the skin, or I'll take yours!' growled the panther.

The hunter hurriedly removed it and laid it down. The leopard took it in her mouth and returned to her place, where she lay her head upon the coat. She wept, and could not be consoled.

The testimony continued until the sun sank towards the horizon, at which point the stag proclaimed, 'We have heard enough! Will anyone speak in favour of this man?'

There was a silence, then a dappled grey mare stepped forth.

'Sister Horse, speak!'

'He's good to my brother.'

She hesitated and then continued, 'He treats Umballa well.'

'Thank you, Sister Horse!'

She shook her head nervously, turned and trotted off.

The stag addressed the hunter thus: 'You have been tried by this court, and found guilty of killing wantonly, taking life beyond your needs, of cruelty and of bloodlust. We shall sentence you in the morning. Sister Deer, lead him to the pit. Rajah shall guard him.'

The hunter followed the deer. He didn't turn round, but he could feel the panther's warm breath on his neck and hear the pad of his giant paws on the earth.

They came to a deep, narrow hole in the ground, similar to the traps the hunter had often used to catch his prey, but this had no grassy cover to camouflage it. He climbed down it but had to jump the last few feet as there were no more foot holes on the sides. There was a splash as he landed in the water that had gathered at the bottom. He crouched down, huddled against the night air. His leather boots were already wet. Looking up, he could see a circle of bright stars above him against a deep blue background. Perhaps he could climb up the narrow shaft, leaning his back against one side and bracing his legs against the other. But then he would have to deal with Rajah. And he had no weapons. As if the beast had read his mind, the shape of a panther's head appeared above the rim.

So this was what it felt like to be trapped! Here he was, at the bottom of a pit, unarmed, with no means of escape. He thought of all the animals he had left this way, sometimes for hours or even days. Hungry, frightened and thirsty, they would either die a slow and painful death after days and nights of waiting or be killed suddenly with one strike of his spear.

He was totally helpless, at the mercy of wild animals. What would they decide? Or would he even survive the night? He shuddered at the thought of the panther's pointed teeth sinking into his neck and those sharp claws tearing at his flesh.

Other animals came to peer at him. At one point some monkeys pelted him with nuts and then ran off, chattering with laughter. He tried to gather the nuts for he was hungry, but they fell into the black water.

He was shivering with cold, starving hungry and exhausted, but it was impossible to sleep because he could not lie down, stretch out or find a comfortable position. He thought of his lovely wife, sleeping in their warm marriage bed alone.

A long night lay before him. He felt like a prisoner, awaiting his execution at dawn. The stars moved slowly across the circle of night sky. Finally, at daybreak, a velvet head and green eyes appeared above him.

'It is time!' announced the panther.

As the sun rose, the hunter stood once more before the stag and the hushed assembly of animals. All eyes turned on the stag as he delivered the sentence:

'We have reached our decision. The hunter shall become the hunted!'

A chatter of excitement ran through the court.

The stag addressed the hunter.

'The path to the cave lies behind you. When you disappear below the brow of the hill, three leagues hence, we shall follow in pursuit. If you reach the cave without being caught, you will be free to return to the Land of Men. Rajah shall lead the pack.'

The hunter heard a growl and turned around to see the panther curling his lip to expose his fangs.

'You are free to go!'

All eyes watched him as he walked towards the path in the woods. He wanted to break into a run, but held himself back in an attempt to maintain his dignity. Once he reached the cover of the trees, he quickened his pace. He knew that if he ran at the beginning, he would have no energy left for the chase. But how did he know if he could trust them to keep their word? Still, they could have killed him last night. But then there would have been no chase. He continued at a steady pace. Even so, he was soon dripping with perspiration.

The sun drew nigh to its zenith as he arrived at the brow of the hill. The hunter looked back to see in the far distance the stag on his rock and the pack of animals. A bellow echoed through the air and the barking of dogs sounded through the valley.

He descended the hill at a run. He must remember to pace himself! There was still a long way to go.

His calves ached and his breath came in snatches, but there was no time to stop and rest. He forced himself on. The twigs and branches scratched his arms and legs as he crossed through woodland. Stumbling on, he caught his foot in the root of a tree and fell. His leg had somehow become entwined in the undergrowth, and the more he struggled, the harder it became to free himself. He reached for his dagger but it was not there. The pack of animals could only be a short distance away by now. He imagined the panther leaping upon him, sinking his razor teeth into his neck, and ripping him from limb to limb with his scimitar claws. With a desperate wrench he disentangled his leg, but as he pulled himself to his feet, he felt a sharp pain in his left foot. He must have twisted his ankle in the fall. Knee deep in ferns, he propelled himself forward at a limp, dragging his injured foot behind him.

At last he reached the other side of the wood, where the trees were more spaced out, and there above him through the foliage he could see the entrance to the cave.

Crossing the meadow, he came to the gurgling stream. His mouth was parched with thirst. He would do anything for a cool draught of water! Glancing nervously over his shoulder, he threw himself to the ground and scooped up the sparkling liquid in his hands. After drinking a few mouthfuls, he splashed some of it over his face and scrambled to his feet. The baying was drawing closer. He plunged into the icy depths and waded across the river.

Gasping for breath, he clambered up the hill. He felt as if his heart would burst, but he could sense the vibrations of the animals' hooves on the ground and did not dare to stop.

As he reached the top, Rajah sprang out of the woodland in hot pursuit. The entrance was but a few paces away. He could go no further. He collapsed, exhausted. In a few moments the panther would leap upon him and tear him apart. With a final effort, he dragged himself into the cool shadow of the cave on his hands and knees.

Rajah stood at the entrance, panting and slavering, his eyes gleaming like emerald slits. The other animals followed and crowded around the mouth of the cave. They parted to let the stag through.

'You are fleet of foot, Brother Man, and have escaped the jaws of the panther. You are free to return to the Land of Men. But remember, we have shown you mercy.'

His words echoed down the tunnels of the cave: '... shown you mercy! ... mercy! ... mercy!'

At first the hunter lay in the shade of the cave, recovering his breath, too exhausted to move. Gradually the sound of hooves died away. Painfully he pulled himself up. By leaning against the cave wall with his left hand, he started his return journey through the black tunnel. It seemed much longer than the earlier expedition. Without the deer to guide him, it was easy to get lost in the sunless maze. At one point he took the wrong fork. The passage sloped downhill and became narrower and narrower until he found himself at a dead end. He turned round and retraced his steps. As his ankle was still swollen and painful, he was forced to crawl along on his hands and knees, dragging his injured foot. When he reached the point at which the tunnel forked, he sat down and loosened the strap on his left boot. He felt as if he could go no further. He couldn't bear to put weight on the injured leg any more, but he didn't want to die alone in this cold dark tomb. Limping and hopping, he continued on his way.

He kept calling out and listening for echoes. A distant rumble shook the walls of the cave. It sounded like another avalanche. What would he do if he reached the entrance only to find it impassable? After what seemed like hours of stumbling about in the pitch black, he heard the faint squeak of bats, flustered by his approach. He had finally reached the cavern, but his exit was blocked! He sank down onto a pile of rocks. What was he going to do? Had he escaped the jaws of the panther, only to die of hunger in this black hole? As he lay there in despair, his eyes must have become accustomed to the darkness, for he perceived a faint glimmer of light high above. He scrambled up the rock face with boulders falling away from under him as he climbed, until eventually he reached a small chink where daylight was shining through. He began to pull the surrounding rocks away with his bare hands, paying no heed to his grazed knuckles or broken nails. He managed to dig a hole wide enough for his body to squeeze through. In a trice he found himself on the other side, blinking in the afternoon sun.

He pulled down a forked branch from a tree and reached for his knife, having forgotten that it was no longer tucked in his belt. He stripped the leaves off with his bare hands and used the crutch to help him limp across the clearing and through the woodlands.

As the evening star rose, he found Umballa standing where he had left him. The horse gave a joyful whinny, and the hunter patted his side before climbing up on the saddle. He leaned forward across the horse's back, his arms around the animal's neck, too tired to sit upright. Umballa needed little guidance as he carried his master home. A light shone in the cottage window.

The hunter dismounted and went to the door. Hearing the clatter of horse's hooves on the cobble-stones, his wife ran out to greet him.

'Dear husband, where hast thou been? I were worried about thee, thou hast been gone so long.'

The hunter passed over the threshold into the lamplight.

'What has befallen thee? Look at thine arms and legs, all cut and bleeding! And where is thy jerkin? And thy bow and arrows?'

Brushing aside his wife's solicitous enquiries, he sank down onto a bench and leant with his arms on the table.

'I cannot tell thee now, dear wife. I am hungry and thirsty. Please bring me some ale and some victuals.'

The good woman brought over a flagon, brimming with foam.

'I have prepared thy favourite dish – venison stew!'

Despite his growling hunger, he hesitated.

'Just bring me bread and cheese.'

FANTASY MAN

Emily dragged the wooden step ladder into the bedroom, and, ignoring a twinge of arthritis in her left leg, slowly climbed the three steps to the top platform, where she wobbled slightly. She leant against the built-in wardrobe with one hand to steady herself, only too aware that, if she toppled and fell, there was nothing for her to grasp hold of. Reaching up, she opened the cupboards above her, leaning back slightly, and pulled out one of three boxes that she had stored away there. Slowly and carefully, she climbed down the steps again, placing the box on the floor. She repeated the process until all three boxes were removed. Then she took out a few bits and pieces that were left – a duvet in a plastic bag, an old nightdress case shaped like a tiger, and an electric kettle. She carried the boxes into the kitchen one at a time and emptied the contents onto the counter top. There were mostly old pieces of china, none of which made a complete set, while some were broken and had been mended with glue. Several of the cups had their handles missing. What was she to do with them? Perhaps she could sell some of them, although they wouldn't be worth much. She could take them to the charity shop, but her car had broken down, and it would be too difficult lugging them on the bus. So in the end she threw out a couple of the broken items, put the rest back into the box, and like a film in reverse, placed all three boxes back in the cupboard, along with the duvet and tiger.

Only the broken kettle remained. If she could find the guarantee, she could take it back to the shop where she had bought it to have it repaired. Returning to the bedroom, she pulled out a shoe box, this time from a chest of drawers. Some of the warrantees and receipts were yellow with age. Some of them guaranteed gadgets she no longer possessed. Ah! Here it was! Guaranteed until September 8th, 2009. That was last week!

The doorbell rang. Emily glanced in the mirror, hastily arranging her permed grey hair.

'It's time I had a blue rinse,' she thought to herself.

The figure of a tall man was visible through the frosted glass. Opening the door, Emily was confronted with a slender man with broad shoulders in his 30s. He stood with a military bearing, as if he had been in the Navy. However, he wore casual clothes – blue jeans and a white T-shirt, through which she couldn't help but notice that his muscles were well defined without being over-developed. He must play sports, thought Emily. His hair was fair and curly, his eyes blue and sparkling, and his features at right angles to each other. He had a dimple in his square chin. And in his right hand he held a spanner.

'Good afternoon, Ma'am! I understand you are having trouble with your electric kettle?'

'Well, yes, I am, as a matter of fact.'

Puzzled but thrilled by his omniscience, Emily invited him in.

He followed her into the kitchen, where he took out a screwdriver from his back pocket and started removing the base of the kettle.

'As I suspected,' he sighed, shaking his head. 'A dislocated flange in the electro-magnetic circuit!'

'Oh!' said Emily. 'Is that serious?'

'Not at all. It just needs a few screws tightening.'

In less than a minute, the stranger had put the kettle back together, filled it with water and pressed the button, which lit up with an orange glow. Within seconds, she could hear the welcome sound of boiling water.

'Oh, thank you so much!' she exclaimed, clapping her hands together. Then she reached for her handbag and took out her purse.

'How much do I owe you?'

'Oh, nothing. It's on the house!' he smiled, his eyes twinkling as he put his screwdriver back in his pocket and picked up his spanner.

'That's very kind of you!' said Emily, following him to the front door.

She showed him out and watched him walk off down the road, westward into the setting sun. For a moment she was dazzled by the light that seemed to radiate around him like a gigantic halo. Then he was gone.

She went back into the kitchen and made herself a pot of tea.

'What a nice young man!' Emily thought, sipping the hot strong liquid.

DAY RELEASE

The prison gates clanged shut behind her. She stood for a moment, waiting for someone to tell her what to do, but the area was deserted except for a few cars driving past. Noticing a bus stop on the corner of the street, she made her way towards it. Across the Hudson River she could see the skyline of Manhattan. It filled her with both hope and fear.

It had rained the night before, and the blue sky and white clouds were reflected in the puddles. She breathed in the fresh air. It was the smell of freedom.

❧❧❧

Helen couldn't believe it when they told her about the Day Release Program. Last week she had been summoned to the warden's office. She was escorted by a short heavy woman with a face like a frog.

'What have I done wrong?' she asked the guard.

'I dunno. Nobody tells me nuttin'. I only take orders.'

Helen's mouth was dry and her hands clammy as she entered his office. The guard shut the door and stood by it with her hands behind her back as if on sentry duty.

Helen had never been to the warden's office before. The walls were grey with paint peeling off the pipes and radiators. The wooden desk and chairs were old and battered. In the corner stood a metal filing cabinet with a couple of drawers half-open. The Stars and Stripes stood in another corner, along with the state flag of New Jersey. A photo of the President hung on the wall behind the warden's head. A computer glowed in front of him, and the *In* and *Out* trays on the corner of the desk were stacked with papers and files. Except for the furniture, the office was much the same as the rest of the prison. However, there was one big difference – to her right there was a large window. The glass was dirty, but through the bars and wire netting she could see the Hudson River, and beyond that, New York! The leaves on the trees were turning gold. She couldn't take her eyes off them.

The warden sat shuffling through some papers, his bald pate reflecting the light from the fluorescent bulb above his desk.

'Helen Springer, isn't it?' he asked, glancing up at her over his steel-rimmed spectacles.

Despite his clinical appearance, he had a deep soft voice.

'Yes, sir!' she replied, nervously shuffling from one foot to the other.

He motioned to the empty chair with the papers in his hand.

'Take a seat!'

She glanced around to see if he was addressing someone else. The guard by the door gave her a nod.

'So, you served four and a half years in New York State Penitentiary?'

'Yes, sir.'

'That's a high security prison, isn't it?'

'Yes, sir.'

'According to their report, you were a model prisoner. You volunteered for the literacy program, helping other prisoners to read?'

'Yes, sir.'

'As you know, you were transferred here to New Jersey State three months ago, in preparation for your upcoming release on ... '

He paused as he searched through the documents.

'January 15th, sir.'

'Hmmm ... You have been selected to take part in our Day Release Program.'

'You're kidding – sir!'

'No, I'm not kidding.'

The corners of his mouth twitched into a barely suppressed smile.

'Starting next Monday, you will be allowed out one day a week, as a kind of rehabilitation into society.'

Helen could feel her gorge rising and her eyes filling with tears, which she managed to gulp down.

'Thank you, sir! Thank you!' she stuttered. 'I won't let you down!'

ॐॐॐ

Helen had had plenty of time to think about what she would do on her day of freedom as she lay on her narrow bunk bed. New York City would be hers! It was like a fairy tale. She could play the tourist, visiting museums, looking at the stores along Fifth Avenue. She could even ride around Central Park in a horse-drawn carriage! But she had one burning desire. She wanted to see her children. The problem was, she didn't know where they were because they had been taken into care.

Gina came and sat next to her at dinner on the Sunday night. She waited until the screw had moved off to the far end of the refectory before speaking. Her voice was normal, but she looked straight ahead, as if talking to the wall.

'That diner I was telling you about. It's called *Joe's* ' remarked Gina casually. 'It's right opposite where the bus stops in Washington Heights.'

Then she lowered her voice so that it was almost inaudible.

'Third cubicle.'

Resuming her usual tone, she added, 'Food's real good and it's cheap.'

'Thanks for the tip,' muttered Helen. 'I'll give it a try.'

She finished her food as quickly as she could and moved off.

The next morning one of the screws came to Helen's cell with a clipboard.

'Springer!' she barked, unlocking the cell door.

Helen stood up, her heart thudding.

'Yes, ma'am!'

'Come with me!'

She followed the officer along the catwalk. Some of her friends shouted out words of encouragement.

'Go girl!'

'Bring some back for me!'

Helen entered the Admissions Office and stood waiting while the guard gave a number to the clerk, who was sitting behind the counter chewing gum. The young woman dragged herself up from her stool and went to an area at the back, where she took a package from a locker. She placed a clear zip-lock bag containing personal belongings on the counter and asked Helen to sign for them. With a leap of her heart, she recognized the clothes she had arrived in. Her hand was trembling as she wrote her name. The officer handed Helen the clothes and told her to get changed. There was no changing room, so she got undressed and dressed under the scrutiny of the officer.

The grey pin-striped trouser suit and the high-necked pink blouse with the ruff at the throat reminded her of the last day of the trial. The lawyer had told her to dress demurely. Then after the verdict was read and the sentence pronounced she was hurried down a tunnel at the back of the courtroom in handcuffs and pushed into a van with wire at the windows.

Now the trousers hung loose around the buttocks and her bony wrists stuck out from under the cuffs. Despite the ill fit and the bad memories, Helen felt good to be wearing her own clothes. They made her feel like a human being again. She slipped on the black patent low-heeled shoes and slung the strap of her bag over her shoulder.

The guard ushered her in to see the deputy warden, who handed her an envelope containing some money, a map of New York and details of bus and subway transport.

'You'll find a phone number in there in case you need it,' he advised her. 'Make sure you're back by 9 p.m.,' he added, looking at her with world-weary eyes.

No-one had treated her with trust for a long time.

෨෴෨

A black woman approached. She was immaculately dressed in a pale blue blouse and navy suit, making

Helen conscious of the fact that her own hip length jacket and frilly blouse were probably five years out of date. As the woman drew closer and stood at the bus stop, Helen scrutinized her from under her lashes. Even though the woman's appearance was elegant, she had the hands of a cleaner.

'Been visiting, have you?' the woman asked, a slight smile at the corner of her lips.

She must have known it was too early for visiting hours.

'I used to work over there,' she continued, indicating the grey building with an upward tilt of her chin. 'Now I've got a job in the Big Apple.'

Then she looked into Helen's face more closely.

'Say, are you that woman who stabbed her husband 12 times?' she asked with a mixture of admiration and horror.

'No, that was someone else,' Helen mumbled, looking down at her feet. She had hoped that no-one would recognize her with her wiry bobbed hair, prematurely grey. She had lost weight, her face was haggard and her eyes were hollow.

Her case had been a *cause célèbre* at the time. The Battered Wives' Association had taken it up, as had other women's groups. She had been taken into custody and her husband had gone into an intensive care unit. He had not been expected to live, and there was much discussion in the papers about a charge of murder or manslaughter. But then to her relief and dismay, he survived, and she was convicted of grievous bodily harm.

A bus drew up, splashing muddy water from the puddles onto the sidewalk as it did so. It said '*Washington Heights*' on the front.

Helen got on and sat as far away from the other woman as possible. The bus started up and was soon speeding over the bridge. The sun rose over the sky-scrapers, casting shadows that flickered across her face from the steel bars supporting the bridge. She felt suspended in air, the water glistening far below her and the curved girders rising to the towers at the gateway to Manhattan.

The bus pulled into the terminus. She got off and stood there for a moment, bewildered by the crowds of people rushing past in all directions. Someone bumped into her.

'Hey, lady, get outta the way!'

The noise of the traffic was overwhelming. Cars honked their horns and taxi-drivers shouted abuse at people crossing the street.

She paused by a newspaper stand, attracted by the glossy magazines with fashionable women on the front. Glancing over at the newspapers, she was relieved to notice that there was no mention of herself in the headlines.

'If you ain't buying, don't touch the merchandise. Dis ain't a library!'

She started at the vendor's gruff voice and moved away from the kiosk.

The smell of onions and boiled frankfurters wafted towards her from a nearby hotdog stand. It had been a long time since she had eaten a hotdog on the street.

'I'll have a hotdog, please.'

'What do you want? Onions? Mustard? The woiks?'

'Yes, I'll have everything on it.'

As she stood there biting into the hot sausage, she noticed on the other side of the street a dingy-looking restaurant with the words *Joe's Diner* written in pink fluorescent lights. Wiping her mouth and hands with a greasy napkin, she crossed the road at the zebra crossing and opened the door.

'Yeah, whadya want?' asked the man serving behind the counter.

She couldn't make up her mind. She could have anything she wanted, but she was overwhelmed by the array of choices on display. He sighed impatiently and went on to the next customer. Then he turned back to her.

'I'll have a cheese Danish and a cup of coffee.'

'What kinda cawfee d'ya want? Black, espresso, cappuccino, latte, mocha, light or regular?'

'I'll have a regular,' she stammered.

She paid for her breakfast at the cash desk with the money the prison warden had given her for her day out. 'Pocket money' they called it.

She sat down at a small table next to the window. Cars and yellow taxis drove by as fast as they could in the rush hour traffic. And hundreds of people, mostly well dressed, hurried past on their way to work. They all walked so fast. She looked around at the diner. She was the only white person there. With her baggy clothes and steel-grey hair, she stood out like a sore thumb. People probably thought she was just some crazy lady. When she had finished her breakfast, she walked over to a woman behind the counter. Her voice was a cross between a croak and a whisper.

'Excuse me, please. Where's the Ladies' Room?'

'Where's the what?' shouted the woman over the hiss of the coffee machine.

'The toilet. Where's the toilet?'

'Down the hall to your right.'

Helen walked down the narrow passageway and opened the door marked 'Women.' By now she was trembling all over; her heart was pounding so loud she felt as if her whole body were shaking. Thank God, the place was empty. There were only three stalls so she went to the one at the end. After bolting the door she listened again for any newcomers. Then she removed the lid to the cistern. There, wrapped in a plastic bag, was a gun! It was like something out of the movies. She removed the pistol from the plastic bag and stared at it. It was smaller than she had expected, and fit snugly into her hand. She slipped it into her shoulder bag that she wore diagonally across her chest to prevent it from being snatched. At the sound of the outer door opening, she froze with fear. She expected a guard to come in and push open the door, but of course it was bolted. Two loud kitchen workers were just taking a break. The smoke from their cigarettes wafted into her stall. They were discussing a work-related incident at full volume. She flushed the toilet a couple of times, but they still did not go. In the end Helen opened the door and walked out to the wash basins. The women carried on their conversation as if she were not there. As she walked back into the diner, the man behind the cash register caught her eye. She hurried out through the glass door into the street.

Helen made her way to the subway station. The noise of the traffic and the smell of pollution were overwhelming. She descended the steps, feeling claustrophobic as the crowds carried her along. A Downtown train drew up to the platform. She hesitated at the open doors. It felt too much like going into a prison cell. The man behind her snarled in her ear.

'Hurry up, lady, I don't got all day.'

All of the seats were taken; standing passengers crowded around a pole by the doors. She hung on to it. Although the train was closely packed and the car swung as it rumbled along, everyone managed to avoid bodily contact.

She got off at Chambers Street, and climbed the steps into daylight. Looking round, she felt disoriented, until she saw the World Trade Center towering in front of her, its myriad windows reflecting the morning sun. She turned around to face the park, which was surrounded by government buildings, but which one was the Department of Social Services? She went into the nearest block and asked at the desk for directions. Eventually she found her way to Children's Welfare. The reception-ist gave her a form to fill in.

Not knowing what else to do, Helen put down her husband's address. When it came to the part about her children's names and dates of birth, the tears began to roll down her cheeks. Cherie was five and Dana three when she had last seen them. They must be ten and eight now. Would they even recognize her?

After handing in the form, she sat down in the waiting area and looked around. The ceiling was high with arched windows. The sound of footsteps echoed across the hall as people came and went. A cleaner pushed a mop around the marble floor. The smell of disinfectant reminded her of prison. Placed around the edge between the rows of seats were wilted pot plants.

'They need watering,' thought Helen.

On the wall behind the bench where she was sitting there were posters giving information on various Government programs. They were tattered and curling up at the corners. Dog-eared out-of-date magazines were scattered on the scuffed wooden coffee table. Helen picked one up and flicked through it, but couldn't concentrate on what she was reading. Other people – mostly women – sat around looking anxious. Nobody spoke to each other. At the outer door, silhouetted by the daylight, stood a guard. She remembered the gun in her bag. Supposing he came over to search her?

She jumped when her name was called over the intercom. A blonde fortyish woman sat behind the desk.

'Good morning, Ms. Springer. How can I help you?'

How could she help her? Helen thought. She could find her children for her!

'I'm looking for my children. I don't know where they are.'

The woman leant forward and squinted at the computer screen.

'As you know, they were taken into care. They are with foster parents now.'

'Where do they live? Can I go and see them?' she asked, trying to keep the desperation out of her voice.

The woman almost smiled.

'I'm afraid I'm not at liberty to divulge that information!'

'Not at liberty ... !'

Helen fought the urge to leap over the desk and strangle her.

'If you want custody or visiting rights you will have to go through litigation.'

She had already gone through enough litigation.

'But they're my children! Isn't there anything you can do?'

The woman tapped a couple of keys on the computer.

'According to the last report, they are happy and healthy.'

Helen leant forward and tried to look at the computer screen, but the woman turned it away from her.

At this point she stood up and, leaning on the desk with both hands, screamed, 'Do you know what it's like? Do you have children?'

Helen's face was only six inches away from hers, but the woman did not flinch. She stared back at Helen with her pale blue eyes, the pupils dilating slightly.

'I WANT MY CHILDREN!' she yelled. 'I WANT MY BABIES!'

The woman pressed a buzzer under the desk, and within 30 seconds a guard appeared at the door. Helen broke down and started to cry as the guard escorted her out of the room, holding her gently but firmly by the upper arm. He led her to a bench in the lobby.

Helen had learnt to hide her tears in prison, but now the floodgates were open. The sobs convulsed through her body like waves. Finally they died down and she caught her breath. The guard was still standing in front of her. He leaned forward and put his hands on his knees.

'Listen, Honey, why don't you go home and get a good lawyer!'

She got back on the subway, heading for Queens. It wasn't so crowded now and she found an empty seat. Her puffy red eyes briefly met those of the person sitting opposite her, but he averted his gaze. She must look like a wild woman.

'*Happy and healthy! Happy and healthy!*' The rhythm of the train wheels on the track seemed to echo the phrase that ran through her head. The words gave her hope. But how could her children be happy and healthy? They had seen everything. All that blood. There was blood everywhere.

She had put a lock on the bedroom door, but her husband broke it down. He stood on the threshold, fists clenched, his burly frame filling the doorway. She cringed in the corner of the bed, her knees drawn up to her chin, clutching the blanket to her neck.

'Lock me out, would you?' he growled.

She could smell the liquor on his breath and the sickening odour of his sweating body as he lurched towards her.

'Lock your own husband out of the bedroom, would you?' he snarled, ripping off the blanket with one hand. 'We'll see who's boss!'

He slapped her across the cheek. Helen tried to shield herself by raising her thin arms. She looked like a shrivelled spider with her elbows and knees sticking out at odd angles.

'Please Harry! Don't!' she begged.

'Shut up, you slut!'

He punched her in the mouth. Then he pinned her down and raped her.

With clenched teeth and fists, she fought desperately to push him away, but her struggle was useless. She was trapped under his weight.

She tried not to scream out because she didn't want to wake the children, but she couldn't help herself. He put his hand over her mouth to stop her.

Finally it was over. She crawled out of bed and into the bathroom. While she was running herself a hot bath, she looked at her face in the mirror. Her cheek was swollen and she had a black eye. Her nose was bleeding. The children were still crying, but she couldn't go in to comfort them. She looked a horrible mess and would only frighten them more. She bathed her bruises as best she could and then lay in the bath, crying, until the water turned lukewarm. After dabbing herself gently with the towel, she put on the dressing gown that was hanging on a hook behind the bathroom door. She didn't want to go back into the bedroom, so she went into the kitchen where she sat and shivered. Then she got up, went to the kitchen drawer and grabbed a sharp pointed knife. She tip-toed to the bedroom where her husband was asleep, lying on his front. She could hear him snoring. Then she raised the knife and stabbed him in the back over and over again.

Helen still had nightmares about it. In her dreams her husband towered above her, silhouetted in the doorway. Sometimes the figure turned into her father. Then the knife came down and down. Her children's screams turned into her own as she woke herself up.

The R train stopped at Jackson Heights. She got off. Now she was in familiar territory.

Helen walked the next few blocks in a daze. Climbing the steps, she entered a five-storey building, and stood in front of the lift shaft. The elevator arrived and the doors opened but she couldn't go in. It reminded her too much of a prison cell. Instead, she took the stairs. They were dirty and littered with cigarette butts and bits of screwed-up paper. There was the usual smell of urine and boiled cabbage. The off-white wall tiles that were chipped or cracked had still not been replaced. When she reached the third floor, she walked to 3B and took the gun out of her pocket. Luckily, there was no-one else about. Her heart was pounding and her mouth was dry.

She rang the bell then dodged to the side so that her husband wouldn't be able to see who it was through the spy hole. She waited. There was no sound. She rang it again. Still no answer. He must be out.

She hunkered down in the corner and waited. By now her hands were so sweaty that she could hardly hold the gun. She wiped them on her trousers.

Every now and then she would hear the squeak and bang of the front door as someone came in and got into the elevator. Each time she would stand up, still leaning against the corner to give herself support, and point the gun. Even then, if she had had to fire, she would probably have missed. The elevator either stopped on the floor below or carried on past the third floor. She didn't know how much time had passed. Then the elevator stopped on her floor. She pulled herself up and positioned herself, her feet apart to help her balance. She was shaking so badly that she had to hold the gun with both hands. The doors drew shut and she heard the heavy plod of feet as the bulk of a man came lumbering round the corner. She noticed he was wearing his working clothes. The hallway was dimly lit so he didn't see her at first. Then he staggered back with a gasp.

'Don't shoot!' he cried in a strangled voice, shielding his face and upper body with his hands.

For the first time in her life, she saw fear in his face.

'Put that gun down!'

He made a downward motion with his hands.

'I can't talk to you with a barrel pointing in my face.'

Helen slowly lowered the gun, keeping it pointed at the floor.

'So what are you doing out of prison?'

He attempted a smile.

'Did they release you early for good behaviour?'

'No, they haven't released me.'

A look of admiration crossed his face.

'You didn't spring jail, did you?'

'No, I didn't spring jail. I was let out on Day Release.'

She lowered the gun to her right side.

'So, how've you been?'

He took a step towards her.

'Stay where you are!' she snapped, raising the gun and pointing it at him again. He froze in his tracks and raised his hands.

'Steady on, Helen, I was only trying to be friendly.'

She ignored his comment.

'I want to see the children. Do you know where they are? Have you seen them?' she asked.

'Yes, I saw them once.'

Suddenly her tired drawn face lit up.

'Did you talk to them? How are they?'

'I didn't talk to them – I'm under a restraining order, as you know. I waited outside the house in my car, and then I looked over the fence. They were playing on the lawn.'

His face broke into a smile and his voice softened at the memory.

'You would hardly recognize them, they are so big now.'

He lowered his hands again and reached out to her.

'Listen, Helen, I'm sorry! I often think about everything I did and I'm ashamed … '

'Don't move!'

He dropped his arms to his side and stood, clumsy and helpless, like a giant penguin.

'What's the address?' she hissed.

'I forget now. It was a couple of years ago. It was in Larchmont, a nice house.'

'What's the street address?'

'I can't remember.'

Helen was calm now. She released the safety catch with her thumb.

'It was, errr, Magnolia Avenue, Number 10.'

She brushed past him and walked down the stairs.

Ten minutes later she was back at the subway station. The sun had gone down and the chill evening air made her shiver. She hadn't eaten since breakfast and was feeling weak and hungry, but she didn't care. She sat on the bench waiting for the train. A subway cop was sitting across from her on the other side of the rails. He was looking in her direction. Perhaps he recognised her from the photos in the paper. Automatically, Helen tightened her grip on her bag. He stood up and started to stroll towards the steps that connected the two platforms. The gun! She still had the gun! Perhaps he had followed her. Perhaps her husband had tipped him off. If he were to search her, she would be arrested and put back in prison on a new charge. Her heart was pounding. What should she do? She stood up as casually as she could and started to walk down to the ladies' room at the far end of the platform. He wouldn't follow her in there! The place was empty. She went into one of the stalls, bolted the door and took out the gun. Lifting the lid off the tank, she was about to hide the weapon when a thought occurred to her. Supposing some kid found it and ended up in trouble? Perhaps she should remove the bullets. She opened it with a click and examined the chambers. They were all empty. There were no bullets! She had been carrying an unloaded gun! She looked around for a plastic bag to wrap it in, but couldn't find one, so she just stuck it behind a pipe. Replacing the top of the cistern, she flushed the toilet. Then, with a feeling of relief, she walked out of the lavatory and back onto the platform. The cop was nowhere in sight.

It was time for her to go back to prison. Or she could go to Larchmont and try to see her children. She was in a quandary. What should she do?

She could hear the rumble of a train on the line. She made a decision. If it was an E, she would go to Penn Station, where she could catch a bus back to New Jersey. If it was a 7, she would go to Grand Central Station, and on to Larchmont.

The train emerged from the tunnel.

LADY MAYBERRY'S RING

ACT I

The last of the visitors were passing through the Great Hall. As they came to a huge portrait hanging over the imposing fireplace, one of them paused, as many had done before.

'Ooohhh! Look at this, Joe! Aren't the figures lifelike? That lady has a sparkle in her eye! And look at her ring!'

The woman stepped forward and read from the brass plaque at the bottom of the painting:

'Lord & Lady Mayberry and their daughter, Penelope with dog. Ancestors of the Countess of Porchester. Painted by Gainsborough 1786.'

Her husband whistled through his teeth.

'I bet that's worth a bob or two!' was his only comment.

They moved on and soon the hall was empty.

The late afternoon sun slanted across the wooden floor, permeating the room with a golden glow. Only the *pock! ... pock! ...* from the tennis court at the far end of the lawn could be heard.

Then there was a rustle of blue satin. A dainty slipper stepped out from the gilt frame and onto the mantel-piece, from whence its owner slid down towards the floor. Gathering up her voluminous skirts, she made her way to the chaise longue. She stretched herself out, loosening her bodice as far as modesty would allow, and cooled herself with an ostrich feather fan.

'I thought they would never leave!' proclaimed Lady Mayberry. 'How it doth pain my back, sitting up straight all the livelong day!'

Penelope stepped lightly down from the painting, and taking her stick and hoop, skipped gaily around the room, her golden ringlets flying behind her. A King Charles spaniel with bulging eyes jumped down after her and scampered along, snapping at the hoop.

'Do take care, Penelope,' called her mother. 'Perchance thou mayest scratch the floor.'

''Tis not I, Mama! 'Tis Fifi!'

The brown and white dog continued to run behind her, gleefully unaware of the slur on his diminutive character.

The last to descend was Lord Mayberry, huffing and puffing as he made his way to the chesterfield. He took off his wig and threw it down beside him, releasing a small cloud of talcum powder as he did so.

'Damned hot, these wigs! Why do we have to wear them in this weather? They make my head itch!'

'Be careful with your language, dear,' warned Lady Mayberry, looking towards their little girl, who was oblivious to everything except for her joyful circumnavigation of the room.

Lord Mayberry flung his buckled shoes onto the Persian rug.

'And these shoes kill my feet. It doesn't help standing up all day with a gouty leg.'

'You only have to wear one shoe, as your other foot is hidden behind my skirts,' replied Lady Mayberry.

'Hush dear, I can hear voices in the garden. Someone's coming!'

With this, they all scrambled back into the painting and resumed their positions.

ACT II

A young woman with flashing eyes strode into the house through the French windows, followed by a fair young man.

'I can explain everything, Pamela, if you'll only give me a chance!' he begged her.

The woman turned around and faced him, her fists clenched at her sides.

'So go ahead! Explain what you were doing with Priscilla in the summer house. I thought you had finished with her?'

'I had ... I mean, I have. That was what I was doing,' replied Nigel. 'I was breaking it off with her. She took it rather badly.'

Pamela put her hands on her hips.

'Is that why you had to console her – with a kiss?'

Nigel reddened up to his receding hairline.

'Oh, the kiss! Well, she wouldn't take no for an answer – and then she forced herself upon me!'

'Nigel, I have never heard anything so ridiculous, even from you! I am sick of your pathetic lies and your namby-pamby excuses. I don't care if you are a viscount. The engagement is off!'

With this, she pulled a large chunk of jewellery from her ring finger and flung it away from her. The force of her fury and the weight of the ring were such that it flew across the room and out of an open window.

Lady Mayberry stifled a gasp.

'What are you doing, Pamela? That's a priceless heirloom!' exclaimed Nigel.

'I don't care! You can take your priceless heirloom and hang it on your family tree!'

With this Pamela turned on her heel and strode out of the room. Nigel hesitated for a moment, torn between his concern about the ring and his love for Pamela. Then he ran out after her.

'Listen, Pamela, it wasn't what it looked like! Let me explain!'

ACT III

The next morning, Maisie rose early to clean up the Great Hall after the ravages of the previous day. As she was dusting some of the smaller portraits, she heard the measured steps of Jenkins, the butler. He stood at one end of the room and surveyed the scene. Then he spied Maisie in the far corner, busy with her feather duster. She was a shapely little body in her neat black dress and white pinafore. Yes, a comely wench, he thought to himself. He strolled to the middle of the room, to be within better hearing distance.

'Good morning, Maisie. I'll get Tom to remove the cordons as there will be no tourists today. Then you can polish the floor properly.'

Maisie turned around, her duster poised in mid-air.

'Thank 'ee, sir. Oi can't say Oi'm sorry. Them tourists do play havoc with the parquet. Oi don't know what they get up to, scuffing it loik they do.'

He moved a little nearer, so that he could talk in a lower voice.

'By the way, there's a matter of some delicacy. A valuable ring has been lost. If your find it, please let me know.'

'That Oi will, sir.'

Maisie turned her back to him and carried on with her work.

Jenkins saw his chance. He stepped over the cordon and picked his way through the furniture, which had been arranged close together in the restricted area. Maisie heard him come up behind her and knew she was trapped. As he reached out to grab her she swung around and slapped his face with the back of her hand. He staggered back, toppling a Queen Anne chair. Recovering himself, he rubbed his right cheek, which was red from the blow.

'That was unnecessary, Maisie. I was only trying to help you.'

Looking him squarely in the face, she replied, 'Oi don't need your help, sir!'

Then a sneer crossed his usually composed face.

'You'll be sorry for this! You'll rue the day!'

With his cheek still smarting, he made his way back through the obstacle course and stalked off.

Above the mantelpiece, Lord and Lady Mayberry exchanged glances.

ACT IV

Maisie was still shaking from her close encounter when she heard footsteps from the North corridor, but it was only Tom, coming to remove the cordons. Her heart still pounding, she tried to concentrate on polishing the furniture. She liked the glow of the wood and the smell of the wax as she rubbed it in vigorously with circular motions. Slowly she calmed down as she resumed the rhythm of her task.

The sun had now risen and filled the room with reflected light.

Outside the window she heard the clipping of shears and someone whistling above the birdsong. A smile involuntarily spread across her face.

The whistling and clipping stopped and a tall lithe figure appeared, silhouetted at the French windows, cap in hand.

''Morning, Maisie! How's my darlin' girl today?'

He came over and tried to give her a kiss, but she pushed him away.

'Is sommat the matter?'

'Old Sourpuss tried to grab me and Oi slapped his face,' she replied.

'Then you mid get the sack! Never mind, then I'll have to marry thee!'

He grinned at her with his usual impish smile.

Maisie had heard it all before. She carried on with her polishing.

Realizing that his proposal was being ignored, Evan stood watching her awkwardly, shuffling from one foot to the other. Maisie looked up at him, surprised to see his face flushed under his swarthy complexion.

'What be the matter, Evan? It b'ain't like 'ee to be coy.'

'There's sommat Oi've been meaning to ask you, Maisie, but, well, Oi haven't had the wherewithal up to now.'

Dropping to one knee, he pulled something from his pocket.

'Maisie, you know 'ow Oi feel about 'ee. Will you do me the honour of being moi woif?'

Maisie was overcome with emotion, both by his proposal and the gold ring that he held out to her. It was set with a large diamond surrounded by small rubies, emeralds and water pearls. For some reason it looked strangely familiar.

'Oh, Evan! Oi've never seen anything so beautiful in all moi loif!'

She put it on, twisting her fingers this way and that, spellbound by the dazzling light reflected in the stones.

'But where did you get it from? You didn't steal it, did you?'

Evan pulled himself up onto his feet, looking offended.

''Course Oi didn't. You should know me better than that!'

Then he added, by way of explanation, 'Oi found it caught in a bush in the shrubbery! Foinders keepers, Oi say!'

'Oh Evan, Oi can't accept this. You know who it belongs to. You'll have to return it to the Countess.'

At that moment there was a footfall in the corridor.

'Quick! It's Jenkins! You'd better go!'

Evan disappeared into the garden as swiftly as he had arrived. Maisie was about to hide the ring in her apron pocket, but Jenkins had already seen her fumbling. He had regained some of his dignity, and spoke to her in a cool tone of voice.

'What have you got in your hand, Maisie?'

'Nothing, sir.'

'If it's nothing, why are you trying to conceal it? Come now, open your hand!'

She revealed what was in her palm.

With a sharp intake of breath, he exclaimed, 'It's the ring! Where did you find it?'

'Oi found it while Oi was dusting, sir.'

'And why did you try to hide it?'

'Oi was going to give it to her Ladyship, honest, sir!'

'Oh, you are in deep water! Give it to me!'

She reluctantly handed over the ring, which Jenkins placed in his breast pocket.

'Make sure she gets it, sir,' she added dryly.

'I think you have gone far enough for one morning. Get on with your work!'

ACT V

That afternoon, the Countess of Porchester summoned the staff to a meeting in the Great Hall. A policewoman and a stranger with a wilting moustache and shabby raincoat were also present.

Her Ladyship seated herself on the chesterfield next to her husband. Her son was conspicuous by his absence.

Maisie was grouped with the other servants. Feeling a hand slide around her waist, she turned to see Jenkins standing behind her. She glared at him.

'Good afternoon, everyone. I'd like to introduce our visitors to you – Inspector Hoarse and Officer Byrd. I've invited them here to investigate a possible crime. As some of you may know, a priceless ring originally worn by Lady Mayberry is missing.'

She surveyed the anxious faces of her staff.

'Shall we start with you, Jenkins? You know your staff better than anyone. Do you have any suggestions as to how we may proceed?'

'Yes, Ma'am. You might try searching some of the maids – starting with Maisie!'

A shocked murmur spread through the servants as the police officer escorted Maisie to a side room.

'Does anyone have anything to say while we're waiting?' asked the Countess.

She was greeted by silence. A few minutes later, Maisie emerged, red in the face and crying.

'Oi didn't do it! Oi'm innocent!'

The police officer held up the ring and handed it over to the Countess.

'I found it in her apron pocket, Your Ladyship!'

'Thank you, Officer!'

The Countess examined the ring for any damage and, taking out a lace handkerchief from her pocket, she polished it, wrapped it up and placed it in her reticule. Then she addressed the servants.

'You may all return to your work, including you, Maisie.'

As the butler turned to go, the Countess called out, 'Jenkins, I would like you to remain here!'

The others filtered out of the hall, gossiping in hushed voices.

The Countess addressed the butler: 'Well, Jenkins, in case you are wondering why Maisie has not been arrested, I think you should know that she came to me this morning and told me everything. She has already made a written statement to the police. I waited until later in the day in the hope that you would come to me with the ring. I am shocked and sorely disappointed at your behaviour, after 25 years of service. But tell me one thing, how did the ring come to be in Maisie's pocket?'

Jenkins turned beetroot.

'I ... I ... I ... '

His jaw worked up and down like a ventriloquist's dummy.

'I think we've heard enough, Jenkins. Perhaps the inspector would like you to accompany him to the station.'

'Thank you for your co-operation, Ma'am,' replied the inspector.

With that Inspector Hoarse took Jenkins firmly by the arm and led him towards the French windows.

'I'd like you to answer a few questions for us if you don't mind. You don't have to say anything, but if you do ... '

The sound of the caution was drowned by the crunch of shoes on gravel.

The Earl of Porchester shook his head.

'I'm so confused! Do you know, I could have sworn that Lady Mayberry winked at me? I think I need a stiff whiskey!'

'I think you've already had enough to drink,' replied the Countess, taking him by the elbow.

As she led him out of the Great Hall, she looked up at the portrait and winked back at Lady Mayberry.

FACT OR FICTION?

Lucy stood outside the village post office in the rain. Her attention had been caught by a new ad on the notice board. It stood out from the other cards that were either practically illegible with faded ink, or sepia with age. Through the raindrops on the glass cover she could just make out the words:

THE HIGHWOOD BOOK CLUB

Meets in the Church Hall on The
First Tuesday of the Month
Everybody Welcome!

Contact Thelma Robson
763 661

To Lucy, the notice was like a glimpse of the first snowdrop on a grey winter's day. She had recently returned from America, where she had been living for the past 20 years. While the Cotswold village had charm, she missed the cultural vitality of New York, and felt isolated and bored in Highwood.

On the day of the first meeting, Lucy opened the sliding glass doors to her wardrobe and surveyed her clothes. She ran her hand lovingly over her suit jackets. Would she ever wear them again on a daily basis or was that time gone forever? The texture of the expensive material under her fingers made her feel homesick for New York. Which one should she wear? She pulled out the grey pinstripe with reveres. No, that was too business-like. What about the black jacket with the Russian-style frogs? Elegant but too sombre for a gloomy day. Then she spied the ochre jacket with the big black buttons. It had no collar and was cut like a bolero to form a continuous curve. Not an angle in sight. The shade of yellow was cheerful but not too bright. She put it on over a black silk blouse and a matching knee-length skirt. Pulling a chiffon square from the chest of drawers, she tied it around her neck, lending an air of jauntiness to the outfit. Now for the jewellery. A pair of pearl earrings and a gold watch added the finishing touches. She still wore a plain gold band on her ring finger.

'Not bad for 47!' she thought, standing back to look at herself in the full-length mirror. She leant forward to scrutinize her face. True, she had 'smile lines' and crow's feet, plus a couple of wrinkles on her forehead, none of which could be hidden by makeup, but apart from these her blonde bob gave her a youthful appearance and her figure was still trim. With three deft strokes she applied some bright pink lipstick that acted as a contrast to her blue eyes. She was ready to go.

As Lucy walked into the living room, her mother looked up from the library book that she was reading.

'So, how do I look Mum?'

Lucy gave a twirl. Her mother peered over her pink National Health glasses.

'Very nice, dear. Are you going somewhere special?'

'Only to the book club. I told you about it.'

'Oh yes. Well, don't be too late!'

It was mid afternoon.

❧❧❧

The square church tower stood in the centre of the village. Lucy picked her way through the mossy grave-yard and entered the church by a side door. In the entrance hall there was a chart indicating how much money had been sent to a village in Kenya, with colour-ful photographs of African children and letters of gratitude.

A smiling woman with wavy grey hair and a shiny face came up to greet her.

'Hello! I'm Thelma.'

'Hi! My name is Lucy.'

'Have you lived here long? I don't recognize your face.'

'I've only been here for three weeks. I came back from America to look after my mother.'

At that point, more people began to arrive, so she left the reception line to find a seat at the long table. A tall man with a bald head came and sat next to her. He was wearing dun coloured trousers and a tweed jacket. He introduced himself as Ted.

'I took a writing course recently,' he informed her. 'Did you know that there are only 22 plots?'

Lucy did not subscribe to the 'writing by numbers' school and replied, 'Books don't necessarily have to have a plot.'

'Yes they do!'

'Of course they don't. What about James Joyce? *Ulysses* is about a day in Dublin, but doesn't really have a plot. And *Finnegan's Wake* is almost totally lacking in structure.'

By this time the group had assembled. Lucy looked around at the women seated at the table. She needn't have bothered to dress up. Most of the women wore cardigans over floral print dresses or baggy jumpers over baggy jeans.

Thelma addressed them. This was the first meeting of the Highwood Book Club and she wanted to discuss procedure.

'I've had a word with Mr. Briggs, the bookshop owner, and he says he'll give us a 10% discount.'

She looked around the group, her red cheeks shining like apples.

'Who would like to choose the first book?'

Lucy thought of the boxes of books that had just arrived from America, piled up in the spare room.

'I will!' she volunteered.

'When you've made your decision, you can go to the bookshop and order 14 books. Then we can all go in and collect our own copies. Is everyone in agreement?'

A large woman with a heavy Glasgow accent bellowed, 'If I don't like a book I won't read it!'

Thelma continued to smile through clenched teeth.

'I think we should make it a rule that everyone reads the assigned book whether they like it or not!'

As they were finishing their discussion, a couple of women came in carrying trays with tea served in chipped white mugs and two plates of Rich Tea biscuits. Ted turned to speak to Lucy again. At the same moment she caught the eye of his wife, who was glaring at her from the other end of the table. Lucy excused herself and hurried out into the fresh damp air of the churchyard.

'Is that you dear?' her mother called out as she opened the front door of the bungalow.

Lucy suppressed the urge to say 'No, it's George Clooney!'

She recounted the events of the afternoon at the book club.

'Well, that's nice dear,' her mother responded.

Lucy went into the spare room and started to open one of the slightly battered boxes. She found it hard to select only one book, but eventually decided upon *The Forgotten Tribe*. It was the story, supposedly based on fact, of a 10-year old girl whose parents were killed when a small plane crashed in the forests of Montana in the 1950s. The girl was the only survivor and was found by a tribe of Native Americans who had managed to avoid being detected by the authorities, who would have sent them to a reservation. They had continued to exist in the vast forests, following their traditional way of life, hunting, gathering fruit, nuts and berries, and living in tepees. The Native Americans had brought the little girl up as their own, teaching her how to find food and survive in the cold winter months. They also taught her their crafts and passed on some of their ancient wisdom. They lived in harmony with the earth, only taking what they needed. Most importantly, they lived on a spiritual plane, thanking the animal spirits before slaughtering their prey, and regarding all men as their brothers. When the girl reached the age of 18 she expressed a wish to return to the white man's world, to see if she could find any of her relatives. The tribal chief let her go, asking her to take their message of peace and respect for nature to the outside world.

The young woman didn't want to reveal the whereabouts of the people who had saved her life, and so for many years she kept her experiences a secret. When the book was finally published it achieved cult status. It also caused much controversy. Many people refused to believe that any Native Americans living traditional lives still existed. The Government wanted to know where they could locate them so that they could charge them taxes!

Lucy thought it was an intriguing tale, spiced with controversy. She couldn't wait to share it with the other members of the book club.

கைலை

The next morning Lucy set off for Ye Olde Booke Shoppe on the high street. From the outside it looked quaint with a mullioned bay window and an old-fashioned sign hanging over the door, but inside it was little more than a magazine rack. There was one wall with books arranged alphabetically by author from A to Z. A handful of classics shared a bookcase with bodice rippers. Post cards, greetings cards and wrapping paper were prominently displayed. The young assistant seemed preoccupied with her long fingernails and did not look up as the bell rang and Lucy entered. This was not the first time Lucy had visited the shop. She had noticed that the assistant didn't seem to like people and wasn't interested in books.

'She's admirably suited to the position,' thought Lucy, smiling to herself.

Lucy forgot to curtail her enthusiasm.

'Hi! I'm Lucy Manning from the Book Club and I would like to place an order for 14 books!'

'Well, you can't just order 14 books like that! Who's going to pay for them? You've got to get yourselves organized and collect the money first. We don't want to find ourselves out of pocket. Supposing we don't sell them all? Anyway, I can't go phoning 14 people to tell them their books have arrived!'

Taken aback by the tirade, Lucy muttered something about speaking to Thelma, nearly knocking over the post card display as she left.

She called Thelma and told her what had happened. Thelma said she was going to see Mr. Briggs that afternoon at choir practice and would discuss it with him then.

'Does he know that his assistant is trying to frighten away customers?' Lucy asked.

'Probably not,' replied Thelma, 'but I don't want to lose his good will.'

'We're the ones bringing him more business! He should be the one worrying about OUR good will. I've never heard of a book shop that didn't want to sell books!'

Later on, Lucy received an e-mail from Thelma to say that she had placed the order, and that members could collect their books and pay for them individually.

ॐॐॐ

On the day of the next meeting, Thelma greeted her at the door again with a creamy smile. Some of the members had already arrived. Lucy carefully chose her seat on the opposite end of the table this time, away from Ted. The room soon filled up.

Thelma, who was sitting next to her, turned to her and said, 'When I read the back cover, my heart sank. But in fact it was a very easy book to read, and I finished it in a couple of sittings. However, I thought it was a light book, nothing more.'

Lucy was stunned. How could the quasi-obliteration of indigenous tribes through the destruction of the land and their culture be considered light? Perhaps she had come to the wrong place. Before she could reply, Ted chimed in. He pulled out a thick paperback from under the table.

'I've just read this book about the early days of Communism in Russia, and it was very moving. When the author described snow, it made me feel cold. I didn't think the descriptions in *The Forgotten Tribe* were of a high literary standard.'

'If I was looking for brilliant descriptive narrative, I would have chosen Charles Dickens or Annie Proulx,' replied Lucy.

The only other man in the room, who was thin with wispy grey hair, agreed with him.

'I didn't like it. In fact, I didn't finish reading it.'

'You didn't finish reading it?' repeated Thelma, raising her eyebrows.

'No, after three chapters, I gave the book to my wife, and told her to throw it away!'

'I hope she put it in a recycling bin!' replied Lucy.

Then followed a heated debate as to whether the book was true or not.

Lucy tried to defend the book.

'I tend to have an open mind. To me it doesn't matter whether it is true or not. Some people think *The Da Vinci Code* is a true story!'

'But it says in the prologue that it's true!' piped up a mousy-looking woman.

'There is such a thing as artistic licence,' responded Lucy. 'When you read a book, you sometimes have to suspend your judgement. Otherwise you miss the point of what the author is trying to say. The important thing is the content. It tells you about Native Americans, their way of life, and how they have lived close to the land in harmony with nature for thousands of years. Now their very existence is in peril.'

A tall woman sitting next to Thelma drew herself up. She had a doll's mouth. It was the smallest mouth Lucy had ever seen. Perhaps as a girl she had been pretty, but now, as an older woman, it looked odd on her, especially as she had a hard look in her eyes.

'I read that Indians didn't give secret information to women, so the book can't be true.'

'What about the Cherokee Nation?' countered Lucy. 'Wilma Mankiller is the Chief of the second largest tribe in North America. So these rules obviously differ from tribe to tribe.'

Doll's Mouth pursed her tiny lips.

'I read on the Internet that Running Deer of the Cheyenne has refuted this story. He and his people are angry that the writer has written this book, and they feel it is an insult to the indigenous peoples of America.'

Thelma turned to Lucy again, and with a hint of pity, asked, 'What made you choose the book?'

'Because it's about survival.'

'You couldn't survive under those conditions!' a Scottish voice interrupted.

'It's about the survival of the young girl, and the survival of the Native Americans. It wasn't Government policy to destroy their culture, but the early settlers knew that if they undermined their way of life, they would defeat the Native Americans. That's why they slaughtered millions of buffalo – and do you know how they did it?' Lucy's voice rose in pitch and volume. 'They drove them over the edge of a cliff! Now most of the Native Americans live on reservations, where there is little or no chance for them to hunt for their food. They are poor and unemployment is high. They also have a tendency towards alcoholism. The present Government is trying to help them by providing them with casinos to run!'

A voice from the other end of the table spoke up.

'Apparently it is a bestseller in America. It has been at the top of the New York Times Review of Books bestseller list for 25 weeks!' A murmur of surprise ran through the group.

The Scottish woman replied, 'What do they know? They voted for George Bush!'

Everyone laughed except Lucy.

Realizing that the game was lost, she turned to Thelma with quiet dignity and said, 'The book is about conservation, the assimilation of indigenous people into the mainstream, and the gradual destruction of the Native Americans and their traditional way of life. Anyone who considers those subjects as 'light' is both morally and spiritually bereft.'

With that she put her book in her brief case, snapped the clasp shut and walked towards the door. At that moment, two women bearing trays of steaming liquid entered the room. Lucy stood back to let them pass.

Outside the light drizzle cooled her flushed cheeks. When she reached the bungalow, she opened the door as quietly as possible.

'Is that you, dear?' called a voice from the living room.

'No, Mum, it's Genghis Khan,' she muttered.

'What did you say dear?'

'Nothing, Mother.'

She went to her room and closed the door. Then she took out her laptop and began to type …

GANGSTA GRANNIE

They call me Gangsta Grannie
I'm your sister in the hood
You'll see me on street corners
In your neighbourhood

I ride a motorcycle
'Cos I like to have some fun
Move over Marlon Brando 'cos
I'm the wild one!

Young men try to mug me
So I hit them with my brolly
I speed off with their wallets
I don't stop to say I'm sorry

The cops have tried to catch me
But they say I'm hard to handle
I had to go to rehab
'Cos I'm really just a vandal

The mafia won't have me 'cos
They say I'm much too bad
Babyface is scared of me
It really makes me sad

They call me Gangsta Grannie
I'm the menace of the town
They say my sins are scarlet
But my motorbike is brown

THE OLD WAR HORSE

The horses stood in line restlessly awaiting the order to charge as the sun rose red above the hills. Occasionally one of them would shake his head and whinny nervously or stamp his hooves impatiently. White air billowed from their nostrils in the early morning chill.

A young black stallion called Prince turned his head towards his companion, a large chestnut war horse.

'What are we doing here?' he asked.

'What do you mean?' replied Jasper.

'We risk our lives every day in the heat of battle. Some of us are shot or wounded and have to be put down. For what? Who are we fighting?'

'Napoleon.'

'Who's Napoleon?'

'I don't know.'

Prince was silent for a moment.

'Do you remember when we were young, standing next to our mothers or running free in a field with the other horses? How did we end up here?'

Jasper thought hard as far back as he could remember, but the only image that came to mind was a voyage on a boat that tossed on the rough sea and made him feel sick. Since then the noise of canon fire echoing in his ears and the smell of blood blotted out all earlier memories.

Prince continued: 'One day I'm going to break loose!
I'm going to run away and live my own life!'

'But you might get shot!'

'I might get shot if I stay!'

The bugle boy raised the horn to his lips and sounded
the call to battle. The infantry advanced down the hill in
step to the thrumming beat of drums.

Jasper and Prince watched as the men in red
approached enemy lines. A battle cry rose faintly from
the far side of the field as Napoleon's troops, dressed in
blue, moved forward towards their adversaries.

Muskets exploded and canons roared above the
screams and shouts from men on both sides as they
were struck down with grapeshot or the blade of a
sword.

Then it was the cavalry's turn.

The general withdrew his sabre from its sheath and
raised it above his head as he shouted, 'Charge!'

The mounted soldiers drew out their swords, and,
pricking their horses with their polished spurs, galloped
down the hill in a cloud of dust. The next few hours
were chaotic as steel clashed against steel. Horses
dripping with perspiration, their eyes wide open with
fear, brushed against each other as their riders engaged
with the enemy. Sometimes a horse would trip and fall,
faint from a wound, or a cavalry man would collapse
over his saddle or fall off, one foot still attached to a
stirrup. With no-one to control the reins, the frantic
animal would turn about, confused and frightened, or
rear up on his hind legs in panic. Everywhere was the
smell of explosives, blood, sweat and dust.

❦❦❦

That evening the horses were led to a nearby field next to the soldiers' encampment. All were exhausted and covered in sweat that was chilling their bodies as the temperature dropped. Some were bleeding from the cut of a sword or shrapnel. One horse was limping badly. His rider, Officer Barnes, led him to a groom, who examined his fetlock closely. After a short conversation, the officer took out his gun, aimed it at the horse's head, and, looking in the opposite direction, shot him. As he walked away, returning his pistol to its holster, there were tears in the soldier's eyes. The sun sank blood red below the horizon.

That night Jasper had a dream. He was in a field that smelt of hay, running with other colts. A big brown horse with a white diamond-shaped patch on her forehead approached him. It was his mother.

ॐॏॐ

Early the next morning, as the soldiers emerged from their tents with their red jackets unbuttoned, the grooms opened the gate to the horses' field carrying bundles of hay. Jasper found himself standing next to his friend, Prince, who started the conversation.

'Dozens of horses died in battle yesterday and Lightening had to be shot.'

'I know. I saw him.'

'I've had enough. I'm breaking rank today!'

'I had a dream last night.' said Jasper. 'I saw my mother.'

He paused before adding, 'I'm coming with you!'

Prince looked up from the bale of hay.

'Are you sure?'

'I can't let you go alone!'

The men finished their breakfast, and after buttoning up their coats, gave their helmets a final dusting. The grooms led the horses out to their riders.

Jasper and Prince stood side by side in the restless stillness before the battle. All that could be heard was the clink of tackle, the shuffling of hooves and snorting. Prince turned to Jasper.

'Do you see that wood over to the left? That's where I'm heading!'

The bugler sounded the battle cry as the general raised his sabre above his head and gave the order to charge.

The soldiers' swords reflected the fire of the rising sun as the horses thundered down the hill towards the enemy, who were waiting in line with muskets and canons at the ready.

At first there was no gap between one charging steed and the next for Prince to carry out his plan, but as the horses advanced and spread out, he saw his chance and veered off towards the left with Jasper close behind him. Colonel Mayhew struggled to keep Prince under check but the horse was too powerful for him, ignoring the pain of the spurs digging into his flanks. They wove in and out between the advancing line of horses, causing confusion amongst the other animals and chaos amongst the men, who shouted at each other and were distracted for a moment from the approaching enemy.

'Where are they going?'

'What are they doing?'

'It looks like Mayhew and Cavanaugh!'

'Someone stop them!'

'Come back – you'll be court martialled!'

The cries rang out above the resounding thud of pounding hooves, but nothing could divert Prince from his determination to escape. Jasper felt a sharp stinging sensation in his haunches as someone fired a blunderbuss in his direction. Finally the two renegade horses reached the side of the field, leapt over a stone wall and into the cool shade of the wood. Their masters lay flat on the horses' backs to avoid being knocked off or scratched by twigs and branches. At last they came to a clearing and stopped.

'We made it!' exclaimed Prince.

'But what should we do with our riders?' asked Jasper.

Prince reared up, and after three attempts, threw Colonel Mayhew to the ground. Jasper followed suit, balancing on his hind legs, but Lieutenant Cavanaugh was a skilled horseman, and was not so easily thrown. In the end Jasper lay down on his side and rolled over, barely missing Cavanaugh's legs as his master rolled to safety.

'We're free!' roared Prince, and galloped off through the trees, with Jasper close behind him. They could hear the sound of other horses on their trail, but the noise of hooves came to a stop at the clearing. Their riders dismounted to speak to the two officers, who were rubbing their injuries and looking shame-faced and bewildered. The horses could hear the men's voices behind them.

'Colonel Mayhew and Lieutenant Cavanaugh, I am arresting you in the King's name for dereliction of duty, abandoning your post in the midst of battle ... '

Once the two horses came out of the woods they headed off across fields, leaping over hedges and fences. But Jasper was lagging behind.

'What's the matter?' asked Prince. 'You're bleeding.'

Jasper turned his head to see blood flowing down his flanks. He flicked away the flies that buzzed around his wound with a whisk of his tail.

'Oh, it's nothing,' replied Jasper. 'Some shrapnel from a blunderbuss.'

As the sun rose higher in the sky, they came to a stream of cool water, where they stopped and drank until their thirst was quenched. There was no sound of their pursuers, only the distant call of birds and the rustle of trees.

'What shall we do now?' asked Jasper. 'Shall we stay here?'

'I think we should keep going for as long as possible,' replied Prince. 'The further we go, the less likely we are to be caught.'

'Perhaps you should go on by yourself. I'm only holding you up.'

'No, I'm not leaving you. We're in this together.'

So they trotted along country roads, up hills, past fields of cattle sheltering from the mid-day heat under leafy trees, and down valleys that provided them with welcome shade, until the sun began to set. Their muscles were aching and they felt exhausted from all the exertion. As they passed a farm, they caught the sweet scent of hay. Prince looked over the hedge. On the other side lay a meadow with a stone farmhouse at the far end. A flock of sheep was grazing peacefully. With one bound Prince cleared the hedge and landed in the field. The sheep scattered in surprise and regrouped in a far corner. Prince looked back at Jasper.

'Come on, it's not very high!'

'I can't. I have no more energy.'

'Wait, I'll see if I can open the gate.'

Prince trotted along to a wooden gate that had a rusted iron loop over the gate post. With his muzzle and teeth he managed to lift it and the gate swung open. He laughed to himself.

'A gate made for sheep!'

Jasper walked slowly towards the gate and into the field, where he lay down on the stubble. It was blissful to rest for a moment.

'Don't lie down! The best grass is further along!'

'I can go no further!'

When Jasper closed his eyes, he had a vision of his mother's face.

'I can see Star!' he gasped.

Prince looked up at the sky in puzzlement.

'What do you mean? It's too early for stars!'

'My mother's name was Star.'

'This is all my fault! If we had stayed this wouldn't have happened!'

'If we had stayed, we would both have been killed sooner or later. This way I die a free horse!'

'Don't talk about dying, Jasper. What would I do without you?'

But it was too late.

Jasper lay staring ahead, unblinking.

He could hear his mother's voice:

'Follow me! I'll take you to the land of the Great Mother Horse, where there is no pain or sorrow, and you can run free ... '

THE MARRIAGE CONTRACT

The sun rose swiftly above the horizon like a golden disc, flooding the plains with light. A buzz of awed excitement erupted to the right of the plane as Mount Kilimanjaro came into sight. Barbara leaned forward to catch a glimpse of a snow-capped peak against a lemon yellow sky.

The man sitting next to her pointed out another mountain to the left.

'That's Mount Kenya,' he informed her proudly, 'and over there is the Great Rift Valley.'

Babs craned her neck to look down at the landscape stretched beneath her. Rivers meandered like pale blue satin ribbons to distant lakes, the Savannah stretched yellow-brown and the hills were green with neat tea plantations. As the plane began its descent, the skyscrapers of Nairobi rose out of the plains.

'Is this your first trip to Africa?' asked her neighbour.

'Yes,' she replied. 'I'm visiting my younger brother. He's doing Voluntary Service Overseas.'

While she was excited about seeing Kenya, more than anything she looked forward to being with Mark again. Despite a nine year age gap between them, they were very close. In reality, she was more like a mother to him than a sister.

The wheels of the plane touched down and the passengers bounced along until the aircraft juddered to a halt outside the Joko Kenyatta International Airport terminus. The warm air engulfed her like a lover's embrace as she stood at the top of the gangway, waiting for the passengers in front of her to struggle down with their hand luggage.

The Arrivals Lounge had a deserted feel about it. Most of the officials gave the impression of having been dragged out of bed too early. The man at the immigration window was still drinking his tea. Retrieving her suitcase from a rickety carousel, she loaded it onto a cart, which she pushed through customs and on to the exit. A handful of taxi drivers stood around smoking, while tour guides waved placards, looking out for their clients as they passed through the gate and out onto the street. It was easy to spot Mark. There he was, tall and lanky. He was more muscular and sinewy than when she had last seen him three months ago and seemed to have filled out. His curly dark brown hair was longer and thicker, and his olive green T-shirt and khaki shorts showed off his tanned arms and legs. He was grinning all over his face.

'Hello, Babs!' he cried as he grasped her in a hug. 'How are you? How was your flight?'

'It was fine. And how are you?'

They released each other and Babs took both his hands, stepping back to admire him.

'Well, look at you! You left home a gangly youth and here you are – a young man!'

The taxi hurtled through the busy traffic. Arriving in Nairobi for the first time was an assault on the senses for a woman used to the calm and orderliness of Tunbridge Wells. It was as if someone had turned up the volume and brightness buttons on life. Women in traditional dress, their hair tied in coloured scarves, moved gracefully along the pavements. Some were thin, their scrawny arms sticking out from their sleeves. The heavier women seemed unaware of their excess weight, swaying their hips proudly as they negotiated the traffic. Most of the men wore short-sleeved shirts and shorts while others were dressed in safari suits. Beggars exhibited their deformed limbs. Cars darted about honking their horns while drivers shouted abuse through the open windows of their vehicles. Mark pointed out the Matatus – psychedelic minibuses that wove in and out between the other cars and buses with no regard to safety or the speed limit, loud music blaring from their radios.

To Babs' relief, they were soon in the business district, hemmed in by modern skyscrapers on either side. They finally arrived at a hotel down a shabby side road. Mark apologized for its run-down condition.

'It's not the Ritz, but it's cheap!'

'Never mind,' replied Babs, squeezing his hand. 'The important thing is I'm with you!'

Having unpacked her clothes and taken a shower under a contraption that dribbled when she turned it on and then dripped when she turned it off, Babs was ready for breakfast. Mark took her to a nearby restaurant. While they waited for their order of fresh fruit and pancakes to arrive, Babs looked across the table and smiled at her handsome brother.

'So, Kenya seems to agree with you! How do you like it here?'

'I love it! It's hard work sometimes, digging wells, especially under the midday sun, but the people are wonderful. They are so friendly and always have a smile on their face, even if they don't have very much. As you probably know, there's a great deal of poverty here.'

After breakfast they returned to the hotel, where Babs slept for a couple of hours. In the afternoon they walked around the shops and in the evening they went to a night club.

There was a live band playing and the music was loud and funky. The place was dimly lit with spotlights on the musicians and randomly flashing coloured lights. The atmosphere was electric with couples and singles gyrating round the crush of the dance floor. Some of the African women wore colourful traditional dresses; others were elegant in western-style clothes. All were adorned with bracelets, necklaces and earrings, some made out of wooden beads, others of copper, silver or gold that sparkled with semi-precious stones.

'There's a good mix of Africans and Europeans here,' remarked Mark.

'Are the white people visitors like us?'

'Some are. Many tourists come to see the wildlife. Others live and work here.'

Mark and Barbara stood at the bar sipping their drinks, as there were no seats left at the tables.

'Would you like to dance?' intoned a deep voice above her head.

Barbara looked up to see a tall slender Kenyan towering over her. He had high cheek bones, a broad smile that showed off a double row of dazzling white teeth and a small neat beard and moustache that emphasized his jaw line. Before she could answer he took her hand and led her onto the dance floor. She turned round to Mark and managed a 'Do you mind?' before disappearing into the heaving crowd.

'My name's Sayid, by the way,' he shouted above the music.

'My name's Barbara, but everyone calls me Babs!' she replied.

She didn't recognize any of the songs the band was playing, but they had a distinctive beat, and she soon got into the swing of it, mostly by mirroring Sayid's movements. He didn't throw his arms and legs about, but moved his torso gracefully to the rhythm.

'Is this your first time in Nairobi?' he asked during a pause in the music.

'Yes. I'm here to visit my brother. He's working on a V.S.O. programme, digging wells. What kind of work do you do?'

'I'm a receptionist at a hotel. It's all right. It doesn't pay much but I have my own room and three meals a day. I'd like to study engineering, but it costs a lot of money.'

The music started up again. After a couple of dances she looked around and caught her brother's eye. He was still standing where she had left him, sipping his beer.

'Would you like to meet my brother?' she asked, guiding Sayid towards the bar.

'Sayid, I'd like you to meet my brother, Mark. Mark, this is Sayid.'

Sayid grasped Mark's hand and gave it a hearty shake.

'Hello, man, pleased to meet you!'

'Would you like a drink?' asked Mark. 'What can I get you? Beer? Whiskey?'

'I'll have a Coke.'

While Mark tried to attract the barman's attention, Sayid turned to Barbara.

'I don't usually drink alcohol. I'm a Muslim.'

'Are you very strict?' asked Babs.

'Not really, otherwise I wouldn't be here at a night club,' he replied.

'So what are you doing here?' she enquired, smiling playfully.

'Looking for a lovely woman like yourself!'

Mark reached across with their drinks.

'Thank you. I understand you and your sister are new to Nairobi?'

'We are, although I stayed here overnight when I first came out.'

'You'll have to let me give you a guided tour of the city! How about tomorrow? It's my day off and I could show you the sights.'

Sayid turned to Barbara.

'Have you seen lions and giraffes?'

'Well, yes, but only in a zoo.'

'In the Nairobi Wildlife Park they roam around in more natural conditions. You can also see many beautiful birds with brightly coloured plumage!'

'It sounds lovely ... ' Babs began.

'That's settled then. I'll meet you at your hotel at 10 o'clock!'

❧❦❧

The next morning Babs took a shower and put on a pink cotton top over white trousers. She surveyed herself in the mirror. Her natural blonde hair curled onto her shoulders, her blue eyes smiled back at her and the pink blouse brought out the freshness of her complexion.

'If only I wasn't so fat ... ' she thought to herself, running her hands over her stomach and thighs.

There was a light tap at the door. She opened it to find Mark standing in the hallway.

After greeting him, Babs turned back to survey her image in the mirror.

'Do I look fat in these trousers?' she asked.

Mark looked her up and down appreciatively, knowing better than to enter the minefield of weight issues.

'You look lovely! Come on, we don't want to keep Sayid waiting, do we?'

They took the stairs down to the lobby, where they sat around in threadbare armchairs. The barman offered them a drink, which they declined.

Sayid was late and Mark started to shift in his chair and drum his fingers impatiently on the arms.

'What's the matter, darling? You don't mind seeing the sights with Sayid, do you?'

'No, but I was hoping to spend some time alone with you.'

'Don't worry, you will see more than enough of me! Sayid has to work most of the time. Anyway, we're lucky to have a guide to take us around.'

At that moment Sayid appeared in an immaculate white tunic over white cotton trousers. He wore a crocheted white skullcap on his head. He was all smiles as he greeted Mark and Babs. They passed through the revolving doors and out into the dazzling light and hubbub of the city streets.

That evening Sayid took them to an exclusive seafood restaurant. They passed a fountain bubbling away in the courtyard under banyan trees and palm fronds as the maître d' lead them to their table. Babs was glad to sit down after all the walking they had done in the National Park. A waiter brought them menus.

'It's quite expensive!' commented Mark.

'Yes it is, but it's the best seafood in town,' replied Sayid.

After they had placed their orders, Sayid turned to Babs.

'So, Babs, what do you think of Nairobi?'

'Well, the National Park was absolutely wonderful. It was amazing to see all those wild animals roaming free – and so close the city centre!'

'Yes, it's the largest wildlife reserve in Africa within the boundaries of a city!' replied Sayid proudly.

'And I'm surprised to see how modern Nairobi is. I didn't expect to see all those high-rise buildings and fancy shops.'

'The business and commercial district is very wealthy, but of course there are many slums in the outlying areas. Not everyone benefits from its prosperity. There are many poor people here. That is why there is so much crime.'

As Sayid had promised, the food was excellent. When the waiter brought the bill, Sayid reached out for the silver tray, but Mark stopped him.

'I'll pay for it,' he offered in a spurt of generosity. 'After all, you did give us a wonderful tour of the city.'

As Mark examined the bill, Babs noticed his face blanche under his tan. When he started to fumble in his wallet, Babs reached out and restrained him with a hand on his arm.

'Don't worry,' she said softly, 'I'll get it.'

She deftly pulled out her credit card and placed it on the oblong tray. The waiter came over and whisked it away. A few minutes later, he returned, scowling. He addressed Babs.

'Do you have any ID? A passport?' he asked.

She pulled her passport out of her bag and gave it to him. He looked at it with contempt and walked away with it.

'What's wrong with him?' she asked.

'It isn't customary for a woman to pay for two men. Usually it is the man who pays the bill.'

The waiter returned with her credit card and passport and they stood up to leave.

'Thank you so much for dinner, Babs. It is very generous of you!'

'It's nothing. It's the least I can do for your kindness!' she replied.

As they said goodbye, Sayid informed them that he wouldn't be able to see them again in the evening because he was working the late shift for the coming week, but he would be free during the day, and would meet them the same time tomorrow at the hotel.

And so they spent a busy and eventful week exploring Nairobi. On the last day Mark had to catch a bus to Mulala in the morning. Barbara's flight didn't leave until later in the afternoon. The day before Sayid had offered to accompany Mark by taxi to the bus station, and then continue to the airport with Babs. Mark tried to decline his offer, but he insisted.

'I can help Babs with her luggage and see her onto the plane. It can be dangerous for a foreign woman on her own here. She might be robbed.'

'I would be more comfortable if Sayid came with me,' added Babs.

In the end Mark reluctantly agreed that it was the best idea.

On the morning of their departure, Sayid turned up at the hotel as usual, about 10 minutes late. They dropped Mark off at the bus station. Babs got out of the taxi to say good bye to him.

'Call me as soon as you arrive in the U.K. so that I know you are safe.'

'I will. It's been lovely spending time with you,' replied Barbara. 'Take care of yourself and I'll see you at Christmas.'

Babs watched him lope off towards the ticket office, his brown leather bag slung over his shoulder. She got back in the taxi and they headed towards the airport. They arrived in plenty of time for her flight, so they went to a snack bar to have something to eat.

'It's good to have some time together alone,' remarked Sayid.

Babs smiled at him across the table.

'Can I ask you a personal question?' he asked.

She shrugged, still smiling.

'It depends what it is!'

If you don't mind me asking, how old are you?'

Babs blushed.

'I'm 29,' she lied.

'Why isn't a beautiful lady like yourself married?'

Babs sighed.

'I suppose I was too busy looking after my family. My mother died when I was 16 so I helped my father to raise Mark. I was like a second mother to him. That's why we're so close. Then my father was diagnosed with lung cancer so I nursed him until he passed away, just over a year ago.'

As tears sprang to her eyes, she pulled a tissue from her bag and wiped her nose.

'I'm sorry to bring back painful memories,' remarked Sayid, reaching across the table and touching her forearm.

'Perhaps you and I have something in common. I also help my family. I have three younger sisters and two brothers at home. I send most of what I earn home to support them.'

Babs smiled at him through her tears.

'I can tell you are a good man, Sayid.'

Sayid looked at his watch.

'It's nearly time for you to go,' he commented.

'It's been wonderful meeting you, Sayid. Thank you for looking after us and showing us the town. Perhaps I can return the favour one day. You would be very welcome to visit me if you ever came to England.'

'That's very kind of you. It has been my dream to visit England. They have very good engineering schools there. I have heard that a British education is the best in the world!'

'Well, you would need a visa to study in the U.K., and you would have to pay for your course, but perhaps you could get a Government grant!'

'Well, we'll see,' he replied. 'I'm so glad I met you and we must keep in touch.'

Babs pulled out a business card with her contact details on it while Sayid scribbled his e-mail address on a paper napkin.

He pushed her trolley towards the check-in desk and accompanied her to the security gate. He had never touched her or tried to kiss her during the whole time they had been together. Perhaps it was a Muslim thing of not showing affection to women in public. She felt like flinging her arms around him but she restrained herself.

When it was time to part, he gave her one of his big smiles and looked at her warmly in the eyes.

'Goodbye. Have a safe journey and keep in touch!'

'Goodbye, and thanks again for everything! I'll e-mail you as soon as I get home.'

With that she turned and walked away with her hand luggage. There were tears in her eyes, but her heart singing.

❦

Babs unlocked the door to her 2-bedroom flat and tottered in with her suitcases.

'It's good to be home,' she said to herself, kicking off her high-heeled shoes and collapsing on the sofa.

But over the next few days she found herself missing the blue skies and the colour and excitement of Nairobi. The sky was always grey here and life was a bit dull. Most of all she missed Sayid.

The phone rang. It was her friend Jane.

'Hello, Babs! How are you? I just wanted to find out how you enjoyed your holiday?'

'Hello, Jane. I had a fabulous time! It was lovely seeing Mark again. He's turned into a real young man! We met this man called Sayid, and he was so kind. He took us out every day and showed us around.'

'What was he like? Tall, dark and handsome, I hope!'

'Well, he was, as a matter of fact. He's 26 years old and wants to study engineering.'

'So, was there any romance?'

'Not really. Well, Mark was there all the time, and Sayid behaved like a real gentleman.'

'Perhaps he's gay!'

Babs laughed.

'I don't think so! Anyway, I'll soon find out. He's coming over for a visit next month!'

'Well, that's exciting! Is he going to stay in your flat?'

'Well yes. He can't afford a hotel.'

'Be careful, Babs. Haven't you heard these stories about women who marry men they meet on holiday? The men only want to get a British passport, and once they've got it, they abandon the woman, taking all her money.'

'Well, I haven't got any money!'

'But you've got that lovely flat!'

'It's not mine yet. I'm still paying the mortgage.'

'Just take my advice. Don't let him get his hands on your assets!'

'Don't be cheeky, Jane!'

After Babs put the phone down she felt as if her nose had been put out of joint. She thought that Jane could have been more encouraging, instead of putting a damper on everything. Still, Sayid would be here in a few weeks, so she'd just play it by ear.

❧❦❧

A couple of months later, Babs received a phone call from her brother.

'Hello, Mark! It's lovely to hear your voice. How are you?'

'I'm fine, Sis. How are you? I just got your e-mail.'

'Isn't it wonderful! Sayid and I are getting married!'

There was a silence at the other end of the line.

'Well, aren't you going to congratulate me?'

'Of course, but do you think it's really a good idea? You hardly know him!'

'He's been living here for a month now and I've got to know him very well.'

'But you know nothing of his background or his family. He might already be married!'

'Of course he isn't. He would have told me if he were.'

'Listen, find out where his family live. On my next break I'll go and visit them.'

'Well, if you really think it's necessary. He might think you're spying on him.'

'I am, but if he's got nothing to hide, he won't mind, will he? Anyway, he's already met your family!'

৵৽ঔৎ৶

The next morning Babs picked up some small trinkets while she was out doing her errands. When she got home, Sayid was sitting around on the couch, waiting for her to cook lunch.

'So, did you meet anyone interesting while you were out shopping?' he asked.

'No, not really. Oh, by the way, I bought some small gifts to send to your family – scarves, bracelets, that sort of thing. Can you let me have their address?'

'Oh that's all right. I've got some things to send them too. Leave your presents on the desk and I'll put them in the parcel.'

That afternoon Babs noticed Sayid packing a few items into a cardboard box and wrapping it in brown paper.

'Would you like me to post it for you?' she volunteered. 'I have to go to the Post Office to mail some letters tomorrow morning.'

'Don't worry about it,' Sayid replied. 'I'm going in to London tomorrow. I'll post it on my way to the train station.'

That night, when Sayid had gone into the bathroom to brush his teeth, Babs sneaked out into the hallway. She found his bag hanging on a hook next to the door. Opening it up, she reached in and pulled out the packet. She memorized the name of the village and slid the package back in the bag. When she heard the bathroom door open she hurried into the kitchen and wrote the address on a pad before she forgot it.

'Are you coming to bed now?' called Sayid from the bedroom.

'In a minute. I'm just tidying up in the kitchen.'

❧⋙⋘❧

The sun was already sinking when the train pulled out of Nairobi Station. The lamps along the corridor flickered on and glowed dimly as Mark made his way to his sleeping compartment. He had booked a second class carriage, which consisted of four bunk beds. A tall black man with hair greying at the temples was already there unpacking his few belongings when Mark arrived. He glanced cautiously at Mark as he entered, made a grunting sound by way of greeting, and carried on laying out his toiletries on the upper bunk.

Mark introduced himself, holding out his hand.

The tall man turned to him and shook his hand.

'My name's Jamal,' he replied coolly.

After Mark had taken out a few basic items from his back-pack and arranged them on the other top bunk, he stood by the open window.

On the edge of a valley a shanty town came into view, the corrugated roofs of the make-shift huts over-lapping each other as they stretched for miles down and along the valley floor without a break.

'That's Mathare,' Jamal commented drily. 'It's a slum.' As if he didn't know.

'Could you tell me where the dining car is?' Mark asked.

'Yes, it's down the corridor to the left.'

'Would you care to join me for dinner?'

The surly look on Jamal's face melted into a smile, revealing a set of large teeth and crinkles at the eyes.

They passed along the corridor to the dining car, which still retained some of its elegance, but the original wood panelling could have done with a polish. The tables were set with white linen tablecloths and cloth napkins, but there were holes in the carpeting. It must have been very grand in its early days, Mark thought to himself, but he couldn't help noticing that the silverware didn't match. However, all was forgotten when the food arrived.

'Are you going to Kisumu?' he asked his companion.

'Yes. I'm going to visit my family. Are you going on safari?'

'Sort of. I'm doing V.S.O. and had a few days off, so I thought I'd take the opportunity to see some of the wildlife.'

The waiter brought them the menu. After they had placed their order, Jamal addressed him.

'So Mark,' he asked, 'is this your first time on the snake train, as the locals call it?'

'Yes, it is. It's grander than I expected, I must admit.'

'It was built by the British of course, and was really the first step in colonisation. It ran from Mombasa on the coast to Kisumu on Lake Victoria, and then continued to Kampala in Uganda. That's why it was called the Ugandan Railway, but of course almost all of the track is in Kenya, so they changed the name to the Kenya and Uganda Railways. It's known by the British as the Lunatic Express!'

Jamal laughed as he dabbed the side of his mouth with his napkin.

'Why is that?' enquired Mark.

'It was a huge engineering project, the largest and most daring of its time, and built at great expense to the British taxpayer. When it was finished, there were no passengers to fill it! So they invited English people to buy up tracts of land and grow tea and coffee. You must be familiar with the story. First come the explorers, then the missionaries, then settlers and traders, then a foreign government that is bent on controlling its interests.'

'There must have been some good that came out of the railway. What about employment?'

'The British didn't think that the native people had the expertise, so they brought in Indians who did most of the work. Thousands of people died during the construction of the railroad – from disease and accidents. Some were killed by man-eating lions!'

Mark looked up from his meal with concern on his face.

'Lions?'

'Yes, one lion dragged a man from his tent and devoured him. Only his head was left.'

Mark looked down at his meat dish. All of a sudden it didn't seem as appetising as it had been before.

'Of course, it has opened up Kenya to urbanization. Now people like myself can work in Nairobi and return to their families when they have the opportunity. And the tourist trade boomed. Many white people came at the beginning of the last century to go on safari and hunt big game. Why, even Theodore Roosevelt rode on this train! He spent most of his time on the viewing deck at the front, where he could see herds of elephants and lions. And he wasn't the only American president to visit Kenya. Barak Obama came out to visit his family when he was a young man. You know that his father was from here, of course. In fact, he might have sat in the very seat that you are occupying now!'

Mark paused with his fork halfway to his mouth to look at him. They both burst out laughing.

'People still come here on safari, of course,' continued Jamal, 'but they're not allowed to shoot the animals – only with their cameras!'

After their meal they sat talking and drinking. It was a warm night, and Mark found the cold beer that he was served refreshing.

Later on they returned to their compartment. Mark was relieved to see that no-one else had arrived. The area would have been cramped if they had had to share their space with anyone else. While Jamal was getting ready for bed, Mark lit a cigarette and stood looking out of the open window. The moon was almost full and a myriad stars exploded in splashes of light like a van Gogh painting. On the valley floor, dark shapes moved silently. He couldn't tell if the shadow creatures were prey or predator, but the story about the lion made him shiver.

He shut the window and climbed onto the bunk. The bed was narrow, but the sheets were clean and cool. Soon he was lulled to sleep by the rocking motion of the train.

The next morning Mark was woken up early by the heat and light of the rising sun. He and Jamal went for breakfast together. Afterwards they packed up their few belongings and waited to arrive in Kisumu. The train drew into the station soon after 10 a.m. Mark shook hands with Jamal, who wished him a pleasant stay.

His companion set off towards the bus station with some of the other passengers. Mark looked around for a taxi to take him to his final destination. He spotted a man in his thirties leaning on a battered black Ford, his curly hair smoothed into waves with the help of hair oil, his hairless chest revealed by a cotton plaid shirt unbuttoned almost to the waist.

'Do you speak English?' Mark asked.

'I certainly do,' replied the driver.

'And Swahili?'

'Of course.'

'I need someone to act as a translator. Could you do that?'

'No problem,' answered the man.

They agreed to a price and shook hands on it.

'My name's Sam, by the way!' the driver announced as Mark slid into the front seat of the car.

They soon left the city and were travelling along a paved country road towards the low hills that surrounded Kisumu. Now and again they would hit a pothole. Soon the high-rise buildings were replaced by mud huts with conical thatched roofs. They passed people working in their *shambas* or kitchen gardens. Women in bright cloth turbans bent to hoe the red earth between neat rows of peas while their children chased each other shouting and laughing. After a while the car turned onto a dirt track. The driver slowed to a halt.

'What are we stopping for?' asked Mark. He didn't have to wait long for an answer.

A herd of goats was coming towards them along the path, led by a young boy carrying a stick. The goatherd veered off to the right, but his charges took their time in following his lead. Some were tempted by the low-hanging leaves, others paused to tend to their bleating kids. The driver leaned back in his seat and lit a cigarette, shrugging as if to say, 'What can you do?'

They reached the village at around midday. The sun was right overhead and beating down on the roof of the taxi. Mark was relieved to climb out and stretch his limbs.

The compound was surrounded by a stockade made of tall poles bound together by jute. As they entered, a couple of men who seemed to be standing around doing nothing approached them. The driver explained why Mark was there. They stared at him with a mixture of curiosity and suspicion for a moment. Then one of them turned and beckoned for the visitors to follow. The compound consisted of mud huts with thatched roofs. Some women walked around carrying pots of water on their heads or firewood under their arms. Others sat in a circle on the ground, busying themselves with the preparation of food. Mark caught a glimpse of an open fire that flickered inside a dark smoky cooking hut. Men stood or sat around smoking and talking, while dogs fought over any scraps of food they could find.

The driver spoke to one of the men, who pointed towards a large circular hut. A tall old man wearing a striped piece of material around his waist and over one shoulder emerged from the door and stood, watching the approach of the two strangers. Although the man's face was wrinkled and his black curly hair was touched with grey, Mark noticed a resemblance to Sayid. He was wearing gold chains and necklaces of coloured beads around his neck, together with what looked like a row of curved teeth on a leather strip. On his arms and ankles he wore copper bangles. His arms and chest were decorated with tattoos. Two other men of about the same age ambled over and stood next to the old man.

Sam greeted him in Swahili and explained the purpose of their visit. The old man glanced from the driver to Mark, a look of curiosity on his face.

'So, your sister wants to marry my son? He did not tell me you were coming.'

'It was a last minute decision. I'm working in a village outside Nairobi building a well, and had a few days off. I thought I would take the opportunity to pay my respects to Sayid's family.'

The old man gave a slight nod, but continued to stare at him expectantly.

The driver leaned over and told Mark he should offer the old man a gift. Mark had bought an assortment of baubles in Nairobi, along with a swathe of coloured material. He reached into his backpack and pulled out a couple of copper bracelets, which he offered to Sayid's father. The old man took them and turned them over in his hand, grunting. He didn't look impressed. One of the men standing next to him made some comment, pointing to Mark's watch. The old man's face lit up. He indicated that Mark should take it off and show it to him. He examined it with child-like delight, while the other men gathered round and pointed to the dials. The old man put it on, but even with the expandable wrist band, it was too big for his sinewy arms, so he pushed it halfway up his forearm. After everyone had admired it, he turned to Mark and beamed. Mark hadn't intended to give it away. It had been a graduation present from his father a couple of years before he had died.

'I've bought some gifts for your wife and the other women in your family,' he said, pulling out the swathe of cloth and a handful of bracelets.

'The women are working now, preparing dinner. Let me introduce myself. My name is Yusuf, these two men are my brothers, Shem and Emanuel.'

Mark stepped forward to shake their hands.

'My name's Mark.'

'I have three sons, but they are busy tending the cattle and looking after the farm.

A very old woman approached them from the neighbouring hut. She had a yellow patterned scarf around her head and her eyes were glazed over with cataracts. She walked with difficulty, leaning on a staff. When she reached the entrance to the hut, she sat down on one of the wooden chairs that were scattered around outside.

'This is my mother. She is almost blind.'

Mark took a step towards her but, just as he reached out his hand, he hesitated, unsure of the protocol. Instead he lowered it to his side, nodded his head and mumbled some words in greeting.

'Sayid's wife lives in the hut over there with her little girl, Kezia. I have three daughters, but they are unmarried. We do not show our young women to strangers.'

Yusuf offered a chair to Mark and the driver, and then seated himself on a wooden armchair next to the entrance, arranging his clothes. He called to a woman a few years younger than himself who was sitting outside a neighbouring hut, preparing vegetables with the other women.

She came over, glancing with curiosity at Mark.

'This is my first wife, Saumu. This is Mark, the brother of Sayid's new wife.'

She nodded in greeting. The brightness of her smile compensated for her missing front teeth.

Yusuf barked an order at her, and she scuffled off to her hut.

'Tell me something, Mark, do you have any brothers?'

'No, there's just myself and my sister.'

'And what about your father?'

'He died a couple of years ago.'

'I'm sorry to hear that. So you are the head of the family?'

'In a manner of speaking, yes.'

'So you have come over here to discuss the marriage contract?'

Mark was taken aback.

'Err, yes I have.'

'So tell me about your sister. How old is she?'

'She's 31.'

Yusuf looked shocked. He conferred with his brothers.

'She's very old. Has she been married before?'

'No, she spent her teenage years looking after me, and then when my father was ill, she nursed him.'

'Is she strong and healthy? Can she bear Sayid sons?'

Mark shifted with embarrassment. He wasn't used to discussing his sister in this way.

'Yes, yes, I'm sure she could.'

He reached into his bag to show Yusuf a picture of her on his mobile phone, but remembering in time what had happened to the watch, he thought better of it.

Saumu returned with a bowl of liquid, which she gave to her husband. He drank from it and passed it on to Mark, who took a sip. He had to stifle a cough. It was alcoholic and strong. He took another sip for good measure and tried to pass it on to one of the uncles, but Yusuf insisted he drank more.

'You are our honoured guests!' he declared.

Mark hadn't eaten anything except for a couple of bananas since breakfast. His stomach was growling and his head was beginning to reel from the drink. Yusuf's wife disappeared and returned again, this time with bowls of fruit and some small round cakes made from cornmeal.

'So,' continued Yusuf when his wife was out of earshot. 'What kind of dowry does your sister bring with her?'

For the second time that morning, Mark was nonplussed.

'Dowry?'

'Yes, you know, the bride price?'

'Well, I don't know … '

He looked at the driver, helplessly. Sam suggested he offer five cows.

'Five cows?' Yusuf repeated, seemingly offended by the offer. 'We couldn't take less than 18!'

They haggled back and forth, but Mark was not as experienced as the old man at bargaining. In the end they agreed upon 10 cows and three goats.

They shook hands and Yusuf motioned to his wife, who had been watching the proceedings from outside the next hut.

She came over and Yusuf said something to her. She came back shortly carrying a tray with an unlabelled bottle of clear liquid and five glasses. After pouring out the nameless beverage into the glasses, she handed them round.

'She says that dinner will be ready shortly,' announced Yusuf.

The smell of meat roasting in aromatic herbs and spices made Mark's mouth water.

'And what about you, Mark? Are you married?'

'No, I'm not. I'm too young!'

'How old are you?'

'22'

'22 years old! I had two wives and three sons by that age! Listen, I have three daughters, two of whom are old enough to marry. Perhaps you would like to see them?'

Before Mark could stop him, Yusuf said something to his wife, who went off to her hut. About 10 minutes later she emerged with two girls dressed in their finery, wearing beads, bracelets and earrings. They seemed shy and kept their heads down, looking at the ground. A younger girl came skipping out in front of them, her black eyes shining. She stood smiling, her cheeks dimpled, as her sisters were paraded in front of Mark.

'This is Tyra. She is 15, and Nadira is 13. They are very good girls and have been taught to cook and clean by my wife.'

Now and then one of them would glance at him and look down again.

'They are lovely girls, but I'm not ready to marry yet. I want to settle down first with a proper job.'

'But you have a job – building wells! You could come here and dig a well. The women need one. It's a long walk to the river.'

'I'm only here on a temporary basis. Voluntary work doesn't pay! When my visa runs out I'll return to England. If I married one of your daughters, I would have to take her with me, and then you would never see her again,'

Yusuf sighed.

'Yes, you have a point. That's the problem with daughters. You raise them and then they go and live with someone else's family!'

He said something to his wife and the girls turned and walked off, accompanied by the youngest, who skipped around them.

His wife returned shortly afterwards to announce that dinner was ready. Soon they were sitting round a spread of rice, greens, yams and goat's meat.

From the dish containing the meat, Yusuf picked up the goat's eye and offered it to Mark. His stomach turned over. How was he going to decline the delicacy without offending his host? He knew he couldn't eat it.

'I'm sorry, I can't accept your kind offer – I'm a vegetarian!'

'A vegetarian?' Yusuf looked at him with incredulity.

'Yes, I don't eat meat!'

Everyone looked at him askance.

'Are you a Muslim?' asked Mark.

'Yes, I am,' replied Yusuf.

'Well, Muslims don't eat pork, do they?'

'No, we don't.'

'Well, in the same way I don't eat meat.'

'Is it to do with your religion?

'In a way. I respect the sanctity of all life.'

The old man put the eye on his own plate, looking at Mark with puzzlement and disdain.

Mark made do with rice, greens and yams.

That night he slept on a mattress on the floor in the old man's hut. Every time he woke up he could hear the old man snoring like a rattle snake. He dreamt of goats' eyes staring at him as he was being roasted on a spit. The sound of a cockerel crowing at sunrise pierced his troubled sleep. He awoke with a splitting headache and acute stomach pains.

ॐ☙

Mark was exhausted by the time he arrived in Nairobi. He fell into a dead sleep. When he woke up he drank a cup of coffee and called his sister.

'Hello, Babs!'

'Hello, Mark! I was just thinking about you. How are you?'

'I'm O.K. A bit tired from my journey, but other than that I'm all right.'

'So what happened? Did you meet Sayid's family?'

'Yes, I did.'

He paused.

'So? How was it?'

'Listen, Babs, I'm sorry but you can't marry him! As I suspected he is already married.'

There was a silence at the other end of the line.

'Did you meet his wife?'

'No, she was in *purdah*. She has a little girl.'

After another pause, Babs replied.

'Well, he's allowed to have more than one wife. He's a Muslim!'

'Listen Babs, you can't marry him. You wouldn't be happy being Wife Number Two, would you?'

'Well, she's over there. He's over here with me.'

'Look Babs, I'm coming home at Christmas. We can discuss it in more detail then. In the meantime, don't do anything rash.'

'It's too late.'

'What do you mean?'

'I'm pregnant!'

♥♥♥

It had been a grey afternoon with flurries of snow. Babs was kneeling on the carpeted floor, hanging the last few baubles on an artificial Christmas tree in the corner of the living room, when the door bell rang. She struggled up from her kneeling position and hurried to the buzzer.

'Mark?' she called through the speaker. She opened the door to her flat and waited for him to emerge from the stair well.

'Hello, Babs,' he called as his head appeared over the banister.

He entered her apartment, putting his suitcase down in the corner and dropping his back-pack onto a chair.

'How are you? You look wonderful!' he exclaimed as he threw his arms around her.

'I'm fine. And how are you?'

'I'm great! I flew into Gatwick last night and stayed with a friend in London.

'So you're back for good now!'

'Yes, the assignment is over. I shall miss Kenya but it's good to be home!'

'Well, you've come at the right time. I'm just about to switch on the Christmas lights!'

She pointed to an outlet in the wainscoting.

'Would you like to do the honours?'

As he flipped the switch, the coloured lights filled the darkening room with their magical glow. Transported back to childhood, Babs and Mark stood staring at the tree, their faces shining with enchantment in the dusky light.

Babs was the first one to break the spell.

'You must be starving! I'll make you a sandwich!'

'Thanks. I'd love a cup of tea!'

While Babs busied herself in the kitchen Mark stood leaning on the doorpost, watching her.

'So, where's Sayid?'

'Oh, he's down at the library. I don't know what he does there all day. He probably likes to send e-mails without me looking over his shoulder!'

'So are the plans for the wedding still going ahead?'

'Of course! I don't want my child growing up without a father. I've seen too many women struggling to bring up a baby on their own!'

'Are you going to convert to Islam?'

'No way! Can you see me with a bag over my head?'

Babs carried the tray of food into the living room and set the snack on the table. They both sat down to eat.

'You should be careful, you know. If you marry him it will give him certain rights. You don't want to lose this flat. Remember, the deposit was paid for out of your inheritance from our father.'

'I know, but I still have to pay the mortgage.'

'Is Sayid going to find a job?'

'Eventually, but he only has a visitor's visa at the moment. He needs a work permit first, that's why it's important that we get married.'

'Listen, Babs, I've been thinking. Perhaps you should draw up a prenuptial agreement. But you shouldn't let him give you any money towards the mortgage. Otherwise that may cause problems in the future if he tries to make a claim on the flat.'

❧⊶❦⊷

Between them they drew up a draft document that would safeguard the property, any savings or investments that Babs might have, and any future income that she might earn. Just as they finished, Babs heard the sound of the key turning in the front door. She jumped up as quickly as she could and turned to greet Sayid.

'Hello, darling! You remember Mark from Nairobi, don't you?'

❧⊶❦⊷

When Sayid was shown the draft agreement, he was not at all happy.

'I am the man! I have certain rights!' he insisted.

At first he would not agree to it, but Babs held out.

'If you don't sign it, I'm not marrying you! Anyway, Mark had to make a contract with your father. I think it's only fair that you make an agreement with me.'

After a couple of days Sayid relented. He said he would sign an agreement, providing it stipulated that the child would be brought up a Muslim.

Babs and Sayid were married in Tunbridge Wells Registry Office on 15th January at 11.30 a.m. It was a quiet affair. Mark and Babs' friend Jane were witnesses. Her Aunt Edna came from Essex with her three sons, George, Alan and Martin. Her other aunt had declined the invitation on the grounds that she didn't approve of mixed marriages. After the ceremony, they all had lunch at the Regency Hotel.

A month later Babs found herself standing in front of Jane at the check-out counter in the local supermarket.

'Hello Babs! How are you?'

'I'm fine. How are you?'

'I'm doing well. But look at you! You're blooming! When's the baby due?'

Babs looked down and patted her lump, smiling.

'Sometime in mid-June.'

'And do you know what it's going to be?'

'I don't know. I'd rather wait and see. Otherwise it's like opening your presents before Christmas! Sayid keeps urging me to find out. He desperately wants a son. But I don't mind either way. Whatever pops out!'

June 2008

On June 18th Babs gave birth to a baby boy. Mark came from Hounslow to visit her in the hospital.

He entered the room carrying a bouquet of flowers. Babs was sitting up in bed, supported by pillows.

'Hello Mark. Or should I call you Uncle Mark! How are you?'

'I'm fine. But how are you? How's the baby?'

'We're both well. I'm a bit tired, but that's to be expected. The baby's over there, asleep in his cot. You can pick him up if you like.'

Mark reached into the crib and picked up a healthy looking baby with traces of black curly hair. He cradled him gently in his arms.

'You're a natural!' commented Babs. 'When are you going to have one of your own?'

Mark laughed.

'Well, I'll have to get married first! What's his name?'

'Omar.'

'Has Sayid seen him?'

'Of course. He came yesterday afternoon shortly after the birth. He's over the moon!'

❦

May 2011

As the key turned in the front door, Omar looked up from his playpen.

'Daddy!' he shouted, dropping his toy and waving his arms in the air as Sayid entered the flat, weary after his shift at the local hotel. His face broke into a smile. All signs of tiredness disappeared at the sight of his son.

'Hello, Omar! How's my baby boy?'

Sayid scooped him up in his arms and hugged him, bouncing him around. Babs emerged from the kitchen, wiping her hands on her apron. They kissed each other lightly on the cheek.

'Hello, darling. How was work?'

'It was O.K. What's for dinner?'

'Chicken cacciatore. By the way, there's a letter for you from the West London College of Engineering.'

Sayid picked up the envelope and examined it. He waited until Babs had returned to the kitchen before opening it.

A few minutes later she entered the living room with a bowl of steaming vegetables.

'So what's the letter about? Anything interesting?' she asked with forced nonchalance.

'Kind of,' he replied as casually as possible. 'They've offered me a place to study engineering!'

Babs sat down at the table.

'I didn't know you had applied!'

'Well, I don't have to discuss everything with you!'

'But if you take the place it will affect everything – me, your job, Omar. How would we manage if you gave up work?'

'I haven't accepted it yet.'

'But you will!'

'Look, you know I've always wanted to study engineering. I don't want to work in a hotel all my life!'

'But how shall we manage? What about the mortgage?'

'You said you would be responsible for paying that!'

'That was before I left work to have Omar! And if I go to work, who's going to look after him? He's too young to be dumped off at a nursery school!'

'We'll discuss it after dinner.'

Babs brought in the rest of the food and they ate their meal in silence. After she had cleared away the dishes and put the baby to bed, they resumed their conversation.

'This is my idea. I could carry on working at the hotel at week-ends and holidays. You could work the later shift from 6 p.m. to midnight during the week. That way we'll earn enough to cover our expenses and there will always be one of us at home to look after Omar.'

'You've figured it all out, haven't you? And supposing I don't want to work a night shift?'

'I'm not asking you to work a night shift. A night shift is from midnight until 6 a.m.'

'And supposing I refuse?'

He glowered at her, his chin jutting forward and his eyes turning red. The moment she caught sight of his clenched fists at his side, she knew she had lost the battle.

ॐ

June 2014

Jane was walking along the high street on her way to the Post Office one mild drizzly morning when she spotted a familiar face on the other side of the road. At first she wasn't sure if it was Babs because she had lost so much weight and her eyes had dark circles around them. Jane waved at her and crossed over the street.

'Hello Babs! How are you? Look at you – you've lost weight!'

169

'Hello Jane. I'm fine. I don't have time to eat!'

'I haven't seen you for ages! Would you like a cup of coffee?'

Babs glanced over her shoulder as if she had to ask permission from an invisible person standing behind her. Then she nodded her head.

'Yes, I'd love to!'

When they had settled down at a small round table at the Kozy Kaff with their lattes, Jane leaned across and looked into Babs' drawn face.

'So how are you? What have you been doing?' she asked, more out of concern than curiosity.

'I'm O.K. – just a bit tired, I guess from working a late shift and looking after Omar.'

'You poor thing! How do you manage?'

'It's not so bad – I quite enjoy the work, except that I never have any free time. Omar goes to infant school now, which makes it a bit easier.'

'And Sayid? How is he getting on at college.'

'He is really enjoying it, but he's nearly finished. He's taking his final exams next month!'

'You must be looking forward to him leaving! Will he find a job as an engineer?'

'I should hope so, otherwise it will all have been in vain! It has been hard making ends meet, and it's been difficult in other ways too. When he comes home from College, I have to leave for work. It's after midnight by the time I get home, by which time he's usually asleep. It will be good to have some time together.'

'What you need is a holiday!'

'We might be going on one soon. Sayid keeps talking about going back to Kenya to visit his family. I think he wants to show off his son.'

'Well, that will be exciting. You've already been to Nairobi, right?'

'Yes, but he doesn't want me to go with him to see his family. He says I've dishonoured them.'

Jane looked at her in disbelief.

'Dishonoured them! What have you done now?'

'Mark never paid the bride price, and apparently they feel angry and humiliated about it.'

'Bride price? What do you mean?'

'Well when Mark visited them, they agreed on a dowry – I think it was 10 cows and five goats – which he never paid.'

'You're joking of course!'

'I'm not. African people take these things very seriously.'

'So what are you going to do?'

'I told Sayid that Omar was too young to travel abroad without his mother, so I'll stay in a nearby town while he visits his relatives.'

'Well, that should be interesting!'

Jane sipped her coffee.

'And how is Mark?'

'He's working as a teacher in Hounslow. He loves it! But listen to me – always talking about myself and my family! What about you? What have you been doing?'

'Nothing much. Same old thing. Your news is always so much more interesting than mine!'

'I'm sorry to jabber away like that. To be honest, it's such a relief to talk to a friend.'

'Would you like another cup of coffee? Or a piece of cake?'

Babs looked longingly at the food counter and then down at her watch.

'I'd love to but I must get going. I have to pick Omar up from school!'

❧❦❧

Babs was sitting on the couch surrounded by soggy tissues when the phone rang. She wiped her red nose.

'Hello Mark. How are you? It's lovely to hear your voice. I haven't heard from you for a while.'

'I'm fine. I just called to tell you the news. I'm getting married!'

'That's wonderful! And about time!' she sniffed, pulling another tissue from the box. 'Who's the lucky lady?'

'Her name's Lavinia. She teaches at the same school as me. She's a lovely person. I'm sure you'll like her. I can't wait for you to meet her!'

'I'm so happy for you. Have you named the day?'

'Not yet. Probably in about six months' time. But what about you? You sound a bit down in the dumps. Is everything all right?'

'It's Sayid. He's gone.'

Babs started crying again.

'What do you mean?'

'Soon after he got his degree he said he wanted a separation. I suppose it was mutual really. To be honest, I got tired of being bossed around in my own house! He went back to working at the hotel, where they gave him a room, and he moved out a couple of weeks ago!'

'What about Omar?'

'Well he adores Omar, as you know. He comes back to visit him and wants to continue seeing him on a regular basis.'

'What will you do about money?'

'I don't know. He's liable for child support, of course, but he's not so keen on wife support. I'll have to find a part-time job.'

'Well let me know if there is anything I can do to help.'

'Thanks a lot. You're the best! And congratulations!'

Babs replaced the phone and sat on the edge of the sofa sniffing and dabbing at her nose. So Mark was getting married. Within a couple of weeks she had lost both her husband and her baby brother.

Mark had been right about Sayid. He had used her to obtain a visa and a degree. As soon as he had got what he wanted, he abandoned her.

She picked up a plastic building block from the floor and threw it into the toy box. Standing up, she walked over towards Omar's bedroom. In the light of the hallway she could see him sleeping peacefully on his side, his thumb in his mouth, his black curled-up eyelashes silhouetted against the white pillow.

'At least I have my son,' she thought. 'For all the pain and difficulties, I wouldn't exchange him for the world!'

❧❧❧

A week before the three of them were due to go to Nairobi, Sayid came round to pick up Omar.

'Where are you taking him today?' asked Babs.

'I thought we'd go to the park,' he replied, holding Omar by the hand.

'Are we going to feed the ducks?' asked Omar.

'If you like.'

'What time will you be back?'

'We shouldn't be too late,' Sayid responded.

Babs knew from experience it was useless trying to pin him down to a specific time. He was always late.

She leaned down and kissed Omar.

'Goodbye, darling. Be good!'

৵৽ঔৼ

Babs looked at the clock. It was 7.15 p.m. Sayid was usually back with Omar by now. What was keeping him so long? She called him on his mobile but there was no reply. She left a message.

By 8 o'clock she was getting frantic. He hadn't answered the phone or returned her calls. She tried calling the hotel. Mary answered. She wasn't the friendliest of receptionists.

'Hello, Mary. Do you know if Sayid is in his room? He's late returning with Omar and he hasn't answered his phone.'

'I haven't seen him since I started my shift.'

'Do you think you could give him a buzz?' she asked.

Babs waited, her heart in her mouth.

After a couple of minutes, Mary returned to the phone.

'Sorry, he's not in his room. Perhaps he's gone to visit a friend.'

'Could you do me a favour? Could you go up and see if he's there. Perhaps he's fallen asleep.'

'I couldn't possibly do that. For a start I can't leave the front desk. And besides I can't go into another employee's room – it would be violating his right to privacy.'

Babs replaced the phone on the receiver. What was she going to do? She called Jane.

Her friend suggested he might have gone to visit someone and was late coming back.

'You know what he's like. He probably forgot about
the time.'

'But why doesn't he phone? I was thinking of going
to the hotel.'

'Perhaps you should stay at home in case he comes
back. You don't want to miss him.'

It was a long evening. Babs turned on the television
but there was nothing worth watching. She picked up a
book, but was unable to concentrate on what she was
reading. In the end she could stand the waiting no more.
She got into her car and drove to the hotel. Mary was
still sitting at the reception desk.

'Hello, Mary. He still hasn't come home. Do you
think I could speak to the manager?'

Mary was about to give her a speech about disturbing
the manager on his night off when she caught the
desperate look in Babs' eyes. She picked up the phone.

A few minutes later the manager appeared, still in
the process of knotting his tie.

'I'm sorry to disturb you like this, Mr. Sykes, but
I wonder if I could look in Sayid's room. He hasn't
returned and he is with my son.

The manager looked at his watch. It was 11.30 p.m.

Babs followed him to the lift and up to the second
floor. They walked along the dimly-lit corridor without
speaking.

After tapping on the door and calling his name, the
manager unlocked the door. The room was plainly
furnished with a bed, a chair, a desk and a coffee table.
There were no personal ornaments displayed around
the room. The wardrobe door gaped open. It was empty
except for a few wire coat hangers.

'He's done a runner!' exclaimed the manager.

৵৽৻৶

Hardly knowing what she was doing, Babs jumped into her car and headed for the local police station.

The officer on duty took down her details.

'Usually we have to wait for 24 hours before filing a missing person's report, but as it involves a child and your husband has disappeared, it seems a matter of some urgency. Is there anywhere your husband might have gone? To stay with a friend or relative?'

'He doesn't have any relatives here and I don't know where his friends live. We were planning to go to Nairobi next week. Maybe he has kidnapped him and taken him to Kenya!'

'Well of course if that's the case we're talking about an international incident, which is a bit if a grey area. And your husband is his father, so he may have certain rights.'

Noticing the look of stunned horror on her face, he continued hurriedly: 'What we can do is check the passenger lists for flights leaving for Nairobi. We'll let you know as soon as we find anything out. In the meantime you should go home and try to get some rest.'

Babs went to bed but was unable to sleep. She tossed and turned, throwing the blankets off and then pulling them back on again. The events of the past few hours whirled about in her head. She looked at the digital clock. It was 2.45 a.m.

৵৽৻৶

Mark was fast asleep when the phone rang. He rolled over in bed and picked it up.

'Mark, it's me! Sorry to disturb you but it's an emergency. He's gone!'

He reached over and switched on the bedside light.

'Who's gone?' he mumbled, groggy with sleep.

'Omar! Sayid – both of them have disappeared!'

'Who's that, Mark?' asked Lavinia, turning over drowsily.

'It's Babs.'

'What does she want?' asked Lavinia.

'Nothing. Go back to sleep.'

Lavinia rolled back the other way, shielding her eyes from the light.

'What do you mean – gone?' asked Mark, rubbing his eyes.

'Sayid has left and he's taken Omar. He's kidnapped him! Perhaps he's taken him to Nairobi!'

By now Mark was awake.

He peered at the clock. It was 2.50 a.m.

'Listen. There's not much I can do now. The trains have stopped running. I'll be down there first thing in the morning.'

'Thank you Mark. I'm frantic with worry.'

'In the meantime, try to get some sleep.'

෧෨෯ඏ

Babs lay down again but she still couldn't sleep properly. She would doze off for a few minutes and then the horror of the situation would wake her up again. She got up at 6:30 in the morning, had a shower and made a cup of tea. She couldn't eat any breakfast. What was she going to do?

When the phone rang at 8:30 a.m. she nearly jumped out of her skin.

'Good morning Mrs. Wilsmore. This is Sergeant Wicklow from the Tunbridge Wells Police Station. I'm calling to let you know that Sayid bn Rahman and his son Omar were on the passenger list for Flight No. TK1966 leaving from Gatwick at 1:35 p.m. arriving in Nairobi at 2.25 this morning.'

'As I suspected – he's kidnapped him.'

Babs slumped in the armchair.

'There isn't much we can do at this point as it's out of our jurisdiction. If he returns to this country we can arrest him, but as long as he stays in Africa we can't touch him. He may not have committed a crime according to Kenyan law.'

Mark arrived shortly after 9 o'clock.

'Mark, I'm so glad to see you!'

Babs explained the situation.

'Perhaps we should see an international lawyer,' suggested Mark.

❧❦❧

They entered Mr. Murphy's office. He was sitting behind a solid mahogany desk examining a document against a background of leather-bound books lined up neatly on the shelves behind him. He took off his spectacles as Mark and Babs came in.

'Good morning Mr. & Mrs. Wilsmore. Take a seat.'

Babs started to explain what had happened.

'So Sayid bn Rahman is your husband?'

'Yes, but we're separated. I've reverted to my maiden name.'

'Is this a legal separation?'

'No, we just live apart.'

'And who has custody of the child?'

'Well, I do. I mean, he lives with me. Sayid comes over to visit quite frequently.'

'Do you have anything in writing to say you have custody of the child?'

'Well, no, it was just an unspoken agreement, or so I thought.'

'As you probably realize, it's a tricky situation. Is your husband a Muslim?'

'Yes, he is.'

'Then he may regard the child as his property. He may not have committed a crime according to Kenyan laws.'

'What can I do? Please help me. I'm frantic to get Omar back.'

Mr. Murphy leant back in his leather armchair and put the tips of his fingers together.

'As I see it, you have two options. One is to go via Interpol. Once his whereabouts are discovered, Britain can issue an extradition order. It could take a long time and it would need the co-operation of the Kenyan Government. It might depend on political relationships between Britain and Kenyan.

'And they are ...?' asked Babs.

The lawyer shrugged.

'And the other option?' asked Mark.

'The other option is a less formal one, and may involve some danger. You could go to Nairobi and hire a private detective.'

'And if we can find my son?'

'Snatch him back, although you didn't hear this from me.'

Mark and Babs looked at each other.

'Thank you. Thank you for your help!'

As they rose to leave, Mr. Murphy called them back.

'One word of advice. Don't alert the media. Keep this operation as low-key as possible, unless you want to inform your husband of your plans. And good luck!'

వ~త•ల

As they left the building and walked along the high street towards the car, Babs turned to Mark.

'I'm going to Nairobi to find him!'

'I'm coming with you!'

They got into the car and Babs started the engine. Then she switched it off again.

'What's the matter?'

'I can't go!'

'Why not?'

'Sayid took my passport! He said he would need it to obtain visas for the three of us. He planned this all along!'

'Listen. I'll fly to Nairobi and contact a detective agency. In the meantime you can go to the passport office and tell them you've lost your passport. Tell them you're going on holiday to Kenya in the near future so you'll need a replacement as soon as possible. And make sure that Omar's name is added to the new one.'

వ~త•ల

The Baker Street Detective Agency was on the third floor of a half-finished building in the slum district of Nairobi. Among the litter in the stairwells Mark spotted several used syringes. As he climbed the last flight of stairs and entered an open balcony he wondered if he had come to the right place. Three young men were lounging around, smoking reefers. When they saw him they stopped talking and laughing, and looked at him suspiciously. He took out a piece of paper that he had in his breast pocket of his shirt and checked the address. No. 29 was half way along the hallway. The number had been hand-painted in black, but there was no brass plate or other sign to indicate that it was a business location. Mark rang the door bell. A tall, skinny man with a large head opened the door. He seemed to be at right angles to himself with bony elbows and knobbly knees that protruded from a white cotton shirt and baggy shorts.

'Mr. Wilsmore? Come in, come in!'

The man held out a long thin arm with a large hand at the end of it, which Mark grasped. The agent introduced himself as Suleiman, shaking his hand vigorously.

Mark entered the darkened room and sat down on the wooden folding chair that Suleiman indicated. The agent retreated behind a large desk covered with piles of documents and books and sat down in his armchair.

'I thought I'd come to the wrong place,' Mark commented.

'We like to keep a low profile. Even the police are scared to come here!' replied Suleiman, leaning his elbows on the desk and clasping his hands together as if in prayer.

'So, Mr. Wilsmore, you would like our help in locating two missing persons – a child?'

'Yes, he's my sister's son. He's 6 years old and his name's Omar bn Rahman.'

'Do you have any photos?' he asked, putting out his hand.

Mark handed him two.

'This is the boy, and this is his father, Sayid bn Rahman.'

'Tell me what you can about this man.'

Mark explained the series of events to the best of his ability.

'So you think that the father may be living in Nairobi?'

'Yes, he lived here before, working in a hotel. He has a degree in engineering now, but it may take him some time to find a job in his specialty.'

'And does he have any family?'

'Yes, he has an extended family living in a small village near Kisumu.'

'That may be helpful.'

'And your sister – she is still married to this man?'

'Yes, they're separated, but not officially.'

Suleiman jotted down some notes on a small ring pad.

'I think we have a good chance of finding your nephew, Mr. Wilsmore, but it will be an expensive enterprise.'

'How much will it cost?'

Suleiman leant back in his chair and clasped his hands across his stomach.

'50,000!'

After a quick intake of breath, Mark ventured 'Schillings?'

'No, pounds sterling!'

'But that's a huge amount of money. I can't possibly afford it! Where am I going to get that kind of money from?'

Again Suleiman leant forward on the desk. He had a low steady voice.

'You must understand the situation. There are all kinds of expenses involved. We have many contacts, but sometimes we have to pay heavily for information. In addition, I will need to pay my driver for his expenses, including any overnight stays in a hotel. He speaks English, Swahili, Luo and Kikuyu and has a certain amount of experience in these matters. But more importantly, you are asking me to participate in what may be construed as a criminal activity. By Muslim law the father owns both the children and his wives. If you are considering kidnapping him, you and your sister may end up in gaol.'

'But he abducted Omar illegally in England!'

Suleiman held up his large hand like a policeman on traffic duty.

'I am not concerned about what happened in England, and neither are the Kenyan police. You forget, we are no longer under British rule. Furthermore, my driver may be named as an accomplice and arrested. It could be costly to extricate him from such a situation.'

'And would you be able to help us if such an occurrence arose?'

'No. You are on your own. I cannot be seen to associate myself with someone who has committed a serious crime.'

'So you want me to hand over £50,000 to you, with no guarantees of success. Do you have any references?'

'As you must realize, client confidentiality is of the utmost importance to us. I cannot give you the details of other cases. I can only assure you we have been in business for 23 years and have achieved a high rate of success.'

A tired fan creaked and whirred above their heads, to little effect.

After a pause, Suleiman continued, 'I shall need 50% now and the rest in Kenyan schillings upon the safe delivery of your nephew.'

'I don't know. I'll have to speak to my sister.'

'Of course, Mr. Wilsmore. Take all the time you need to think about it.'

With this he stood up and walked around the desk, draping his arm around Mark's shoulders as he walked him to the door.

'But remember, the sooner we receive payment, the sooner we can start our search for Omar!'

Once again the agent shook his hand.

The three men were still on the balcony. When Mark emerged one of them made a comment and the other two laughed. Mark couldn't help wondering what it would be like in a Kenyan goal. He turned his back on them and, with head down between hunched shoulders and his hands stuffed into his trouser pockets, strode briskly to the exit leading to the stairs.

৵৽৽৵

As soon as he reached the hotel he sent an e-mail to his sister:

Hello Babs

I spoke to someone at a detective agency today, who said he would take our case, but it would cost £50,000! I told him I didn't have that kind of money, but he said he needed it to cover his costs because one of his agents could be arrested. Do you have any savings? I still have some money left from my inheritance, but I was saving it to use as a deposit on a house.

By the way, we also run the risk of gaol if we're caught removing Omar from his African family.

What do you think?

Love, Mark

Babs replied within the hour:

Hello Mark

I'm shocked at the cost. Is there any room for negotiation? I can barely make ends meet as it is, and have only a small amount of savings to cover the mortgage for the next few months.

I hate to ask you this, but could you lend me the money? I promise to pay it back somehow or other. Omar means everything to me and there is nothing I wouldn't do to get him back.

Love
Babs xxxxx

∂∙◌∙ベ

A week later Babs received a phone call from her brother. She leant across the couch and grabbed the receiver.

'Hello Mark. Do you have any news?' she asked, fiddling with the phone cord.

'They've found Sayid!'

'They've what? Where is he?'

'He's living in Nairobi, working in a place called the Sunrise Hotel, where he has a small room. As far as the agent can tell there's no-one else living with him.'

'That's good news that they've found him so quickly. I wish I could come over there.'

'What's happening with your passport?

'They said it would take a couple of weeks.'

'I'll let you know as soon as I hear any more news.'

As she put down the phone her heart was racing. All of a sudden the likelihood of finding Omar became a possibility. Sooner or later Sayid would contact Omar, and the detectives would be watching him.

❧❧

Another week passed without any news. Then one morning the phone rang while Babs was in the kitchen. She dropped the dirty pots back into the sink and ran to snatch it up, her rubber gloves still dripping with soap suds.

'Babs, it's me, Mark. They've found him! They've found Omar!'

'They've found Omar? Where is he?' she asked, collapsing onto the couch.

'Living with his grandparents in their village.'

'That's wonderful! I'm so excited! I can't believe it!'

'There's only one problem. Because he is living in a small African community it will be very difficult to visit him. A stranger couldn't enter the compound without everyone noticing him or her. And an English person would stick out like a sore thumb.'

'What do you suggest we do?' asked Babs, her heart thumping loudly in her breast.

'The agent told us to be patient. They are working on it. They cost us a lot of money but they seem to know what they are doing.'

'I'll come over there as soon as possible. My passport hasn't arrived yet but it should be here any day now.'

'Don't fly to Nairobi. Go straight to Kisumu. That's much closer to where the family lives. I'm going there tomorrow and I'll let you know the name of the hotel where I'm staying as soon as it's arranged.'

'I'm so excited and relieved! Thank you so much for your help!'

❧❧❧

The plane started its descent over Kisumu. Babs looked out onto the white clouds reflected in the glittering blue expanse of Lake Victoria, her heart swelling with hope. Every minute brought her closer to her son! She couldn't help but remember the last time she arrived in Kenya. It seemed such a long time ago, and although she had been in her early thirties, she had seemed so young and carefree – like another person.

She stepped down the gangplank onto African soil. The brightness of the blue sky and the warmth of the sun on her skin was a welcome change from the greyness and chill of an English summer. Mark was waiting for her in the Arrivals Lounge.

❧❧❧

They stayed in a low-budget hotel – the less conspicuous the better, as Mark pointed out. Ten days later they received a phone call. They both rushed to pick it up. Mark got there first.

'It's the agent!' he mouthed to Babs, who was trying to listen in.

'What does he say?' asked Babs, her head against the earpiece. She could hear the faint strains of Suleiman's voice.

'Be ready tomorrow morning at 6 a.m. Rashid will pick you up outside the hotel and take you to Bungola, where Omar goes to school. He gets off the school bus at around 8.45 a.m. And have the rest of the money in cash in an envelope, which you should give to the driver when he drops you off at the airport.'

'Thank you! Thank you! I can't thank you enough!' cried Babs, snatching the phone from Mark.

She put the phone down and they both jumped for joy, clutching their fists like children.

'I can't believe it! I'll see my darling boy tomorrow!'

❧⋯❧

It was light by the time Babs and Mark left the hotel. Babs had slept very little and neither of them had been able to eat breakfast. She carried a brown paper bag containing sandwiches and biscuits. Mark carried a plastic bag containing £25,000 in Kenyan schillings. A sun-damaged dark blue Ford Fiesta was parked outside the hotel. A scraggy brown arm holding a smouldering cigarette hung out of the open window next to the driver's seat. When Mark and Babs approached, a middle-aged man with receding hair transferred the cigarette to his mouth, poked his head out of the window and shook hands with Mark.

'Hello, I'm Rashid. Hop in!'

They placed their luggage in the boot and slid into the back seat. Rashid turned the key in the ignition, and after some grunting and rumbling, the car started up.

'How far is it?' asked Babs anxiously.

'About a two-hour drive,' he replied through wreaths of smoke. 'The school bus arrives about a quarter to nine.'

'Have you seen my son?' she asked eagerly.

'Yes, I went to the village with my uncle, who makes jewellery, under the pretence of selling our goods. Omar was playing with the other children.'

'How do you know it was Omar?' asked Mark.

'I have studied the photograph. Besides, he looked better fed and better dressed than the other children. Ther one of the boys called out his name.'

Mark continued the interrogation.

'How can you be sure he attends this school?'

'We have contacts in the school system. It was easy to check the enrolment list,' he explained, holding up his thumb and forefingers and rubbing them together.

'And you're sure he takes the bus?' asked Babs.

'Yes, I've watched him get off and go into the school.'

Babs and Mark sat back in their seats and beamed at each other.

They soon left the city behind and were travelling along a paved country road. After a while they turned onto a dirt track, shaded by trees. The large shiny leaves of the banyan trees brushed against the car and the heady scent of eucalyptus mingled with the smoke from Rashid's cigarette. Now and again they would pass a shack on the side of the road where the natives lounged around, waiting for travellers to stop and buy their produce. They bumped along a dried mud track for another 30 minutes. Suddenly Rashid stopped the car. Mark and Babs looked at him in the rear view mirror.

'What are you stopping for?' asked Mark.

'Do you want to buy some fruit?'

Babs motioned to get out of the car, but the driver stopped her.

'No, you stay where you are. You don't want people to see you!'

Rashid got out and bought some fruit, and passed it to Babs, who handed him some coins. Then they drove off again. Despite her nervousness, she managed to eat a banana.

At 8:35 a.m. the car pulled up on the main road outside the school. Rashid looked at his watch.

'We've got another 10 minutes before the bus arrives. The best thing is for Mark to wait by the gates. Try to act naturally. When Omar sees you, he will come over to you. Don't pick him up in your arms. You don't want to be seen carrying him away. Just lead him over here to the car where Babs will be waiting in the back seat.'

'You've done this before, haven't you?' asked Babs.

Rashid shrugged.

'I'm just a driver!'

Mark got out of the car. There was a slip road leading to the school gate, and a slim strip of land covered with trees and bushes between the entrance and the parked car. He walked over and positioned himself by the school gate, where other parents were arriving and dropping off their children. The car was screened from the gateway by the shrubbery.

'Rashid knows what he's doing,' he told himself as he stood around, trying to look casual. Some of the parents greeted him as they passed by with their children, who either stared or giggled shyly. Others looked at him with blatant curiosity. He lit a cigarette.

A dark green and yellow school bus chugged into view and pulled to a halt ten metres from the entrance. Girls and boys descended from both doors wearing light blue tops and navy blue shorts or skirts. Some ran along screaming and laughing. Others walked in pairs or small groups, talking quietly, carrying their schoolbooks under their arms. Mark watched in fear and expectation as the last few children dribbled off the bus, his heart pounding so loudly it seemed to shake the whole of his body.

He spotted Omar immediately. The boy was walking on his own with a satchel on his back, looking down at the ground. It was all Mark could do to stop himself shouting out. As Omar approached the entrance, he looked up and saw Mark. He stopped in his tracks, incredulity turning to joy as he recognized him.

'Uncle Mark!' he cried, as he rushed towards him. Mark forgot all about Rashid's warning as he scooped his nephew up in his arms and hugged him. Omar clung to him.

'Uncle! What are you doing here? I missed you!' he cried.

Mark gently put him down and took him by the hand.

'We've come to visit you! Mummy's over there!'

He pointed to where the car was parked.

Omar looked round.

'Mummy's here? Where? I can't see her!'

He scanned the bushes desperately.

'Come along. She's waiting for you!'

Mark led him by the hand towards the bushes. As they approached the car, the back door opened and

Babs leaned out with open arms.

'Omar!'

The boy broke away from Mark and ran towards her.

'Mummy!'

She lifted him up into the car and held him against her, her face wet with tears.

Mark closed the back door and got into the passenger seat next to the driver, who threw down his cigarette onto the ground and started up the car. Mark expected him to slam his foot on the accelerator and take off at breakneck speed, but after a cough and sputter the car glided out smoothly from its parking place and mingled with the rest of the traffic.

Mark looked round at Omar, who was clinging to his mother and sobbing. Babs was smiling through her tears, her face radiant with happiness and relief.

'We did it!' he exclaimed.

Then he turned to Rashid.

'Thank you!' he said, 'Thank you for all your help!'

'It's not over yet!' cautioned the driver. 'Now we have to make it to the airport!'

After a while the sobbing died down in the back seat.

'Would you like something to eat?' asked Babs, offering her son a banana.

'Where were you Mummy? Daddy left me with all these strange people and I didn't like the food.'

'Did they treat you well?'

'It was all right I suppose, but I missed you. Where are we going?'

'We're going home now, back to England.'

'What about Daddy? Is he coming with us?'

Babs hesitated.

'Yes, we're meeting him at the airport.'

His face lit up.

'Are we going on a plane?'

Soon Omar settled down and fell asleep across his mother's lap.

Miss Ubangwe realized that Omar was missing when she called the register.

'Has anyone seen Omar?' she asked the rows of shining faces.

'Yes, he was on the school bus,' called out one boy.

A little girl with plaited hair put up her hand.

'His uncle came to pick him up.'

'His uncle?' asked the teacher, beginning to feel the inklings of anxiety. 'Where was this?'

'Just outside the school gates!'

Perhaps he had to go to the dentist or the clinic, but Miss Ubangwe should have been informed.

'I'd better check with the Head Mistress,' she thought.

But then they ran out of paste and she had to mix some more, and the children made a mess sticking cut-outs to a frieze, so it wasn't until play-time that she had a free moment.

She tapped on Mrs. Hussein's door.

'Come in,' replied a throaty voice.

'Mrs. Hussein, Omar didn't come to school this morning. One of the children said that he left with his uncle. Did you receive a message from his family?'

'Omar al Rahman? I don't think so,' she replied, her forehead wrinkling into a puzzled frown.

The head mistress sorted through the files on her desk and pulled out a list of pupils and their contact numbers.

'I'll give his father a call. He's in Nairobi, isn't he?'

৵৽৹৶

Just before 11 a.m. the car came to the main road. As the sun rose higher in the translucent sky, the inside of the car grew hotter. Even though the open windows provided a slight breeze, everyone was dripping with perspiration.

'We'll soon be there!' remarked Rashid.

About a mile along the road the cars began to slow down at what appeared to be a traffic jam.

'What's the matter?' asked Mark. 'Has there been an accident?'

Rashid leant out of the window and craned his neck.

'It looks like a road block!'

'What are they looking for?'

'I don't know. It could be anything. Get your passports out and give them to me!'

Mark and Babs exchanged glances.

'Could he have caught up with us so quickly?'

'I don't know, but he could have informed the police.'

Babs began to feel nauseous and clutched her child even closer to her.

After about 15 minutes they edged their way to the barricade, which was manned by three policemen carrying guns.

'Let me do the talking,' said Rashid out of the corner of his mouth.

A stomach that bulged over a leather belt appeared at the window. There was a pistol strapped to his hip. A round-faced police officer wearing a peaked cap bent down and, poking his head inside the car, scrutinized the occupants.

'Papers?' he asked, putting out his hand.

Rashid gave him the documents.

He studied them and then looked more carefully at Babs.

'Is this your wife?' he asked Mark.

'No, she's my sister,' he replied.

'Where's your husband?' he asked Babs.

By this time Omar had woken up and was listening attentively to the conversation.

'Daddy's at the airport!' he shouted out.

'We're meeting his father at Kisumu Airport and then we're travelling back to England. We're just here on a visit,' Babs answered, her heart in her mouth.

The officer grunted and motioned to Rashid to open up the boot of the car. The driver got out and stood by while a black and brown Alsatian the size of a wolf sniffed their bags.

'O.K.' the policeman called out, slamming the boot shut, 'You can go!'

Rashid jumped back in the car and started the engine.

When they were out of hearing range of the police, they collapsed with relief.

'Thank God!' cried Babs.

'That was a close shave!' remarked Mark, bursting with euphoria.

'If they had found the money, we would have been in trouble!' remarked Rashid. 'Where is it, by the way?'

'Babs is sitting on it! Do you want it now?'

'No, wait until we get to the airport. If I'm discovered with that amount of money on me, the authorities will be suspicious.'

'You're boss must trust you!' commented Mark.

'To tell the truth, we're partners, but if the cops ask me, I'm a taxi driver.

'When will we get to the airport, Mummy?' piped up Omar.

'Soon darling. Be patient.'

'What's the time of the next flight?' asked Rashid.

Mark checked his mobile phone.

'The next flight out to London leaves at 3.40 p.m., so we have plenty of time.'

'Not too much time, I hope!' commented Babs.

❧❧❧

The taxi drew into the parking area outside Kisumu Airport. Rashid looked at Mark and Babs and allowed himself a smile that revealed a gold tooth.

'We're here – safe and sound!'

'Thank you, Rashid, I can't thank you enough!' said Babs.

'You could start by paying me!'

'Oh, yes!'

Babs removed the plastic bag from under her seat and handed it to the driver, who sat and counted the wads of notes inside the paper bag while Mark removed their luggage from the boot. Babs stood holding Omar. When Rashid had finished he placed the bag in the glove compartment and shook hands with them through the open window.

'I won't get out. Goodbye and good luck!'

With a wave of the hand he started up the engine and with what sounded like a small explosion, zoomed off.

Babs and Mark looked around nervously before making their way to the entrance of the departures lounge, picking up a cart on the way. When they got inside, Mark indicated a long row of plastic seats.

'Sit here while I go and get the tickets.'

A woman in a yellow and orange print dress sitting opposite her kept looking at Omar.

'He's a lovely little boy. Is he your son?'

'Yes he is.'

'What's his name?'

Babs thought of lying, but she knew her son would correct her.

'Omar.'

'We're going to ride on a plane!' explained the boy.

'Well, that's exciting, isn't it?'

To her relief, Mark approached with the tickets. She said goodbye to the woman and they made their way to the check-in desk. No eyebrows were raised or awkward questions asked.

They passed through passport control and security, and arrived at a waiting area, where they sat down.

'Even if Sayid does turn up, he won't be able to get into the departure lounge without a ticket!' commented Mark.

'Do you think he would come from Nairobi?' asked Babs.

'I don't know. It only takes half an hour by plane.'

Mark looked around and spotted a snack bar nearby.

'I could kill a beer! Would you like something to drink?'

Mark trundled off with the drinks order while Babs rummaged in her bulky handbag. Pulling out a couple of soggy cheese sandwiches from a greasy bag, she handed one to Omar and bit into the other one. She was beginning to feel hungry now.

'When's Daddy going to come?' he asked.

'Oh, he's travelling on a later plane.'

Suddenly Omar's arms went up and he shouted out, 'Daddy!'

Babs looked round in terror.

There on the far side of the lounge, Sayid was coming towards them, flanked by two airport police wearing brown and white uniforms and carrying truncheons.

Babs stood up and grabbed hold of Omar, but she didn't know where to run. Perhaps she could head for the ladies' room, but the police would follow her and then she would be trapped. She stood frozen to the spot.

As Sayid drew nearer, Omar broke away from his mother and ran towards him, throwing his little arms around his father's legs.

The three men towered above her.

'So, I caught up with you in the nick of time!' sneered Sayid, black eyes flashing under a furrowed brow.

'Is this your son?' asked one of the guards.

'Yes, and this is my wife, who tried to kidnap him!'

'You kidnapped him from me! If you go back to England they'll put you in jail!'

Omar started crying and clinging to his mother.

'What are you going to do? Arrest me in front of our son?' asked Babs.

At that moment Mark returned carrying a tray of drinks. When he saw Sayid, the colour drained out of his face. He put the tray down carefully on the plastic table.

'Who's this?' asked the other guard.

'This is my brother,' explained Babs.

'Will passengers for Flight No. 540 to Heathrow, England, stopping at Nairobi and Doha, please go to Gate No. 3,' announced a woman's voice over the loudspeaker.

Babs looked at Mark.

'You go! I'll stay here and sort this out.'

'I can't leave you like this!'

'There's no point in you staying. You have to get back to work and you don't want to waste your ticket.'

Sayid and the two policemen looked at him.

'What's the matter?' asked Babs, 'You're not going to arrest him too, are you?'

'Let him go,' grunted Sayid.

Mark embraced his sister and nephew and reluctantly moved towards the gate, looking back anxiously as he went.

Babs turned to her husband.

'Listen, Sayid. Why don't we go back to the hotel and talk things over? Omar is exhausted and so am I!'

Not knowing what else to do, Sayid agreed. He turned to the guards.

'It's all right. I'm not going to press charges. Thanks for your help.'

❧❦❧

The following day Mark received an e-mail from Babs:

'Sayid and I have talked things over and we have
agreed that I should stay here and look after Omar
while he works. He hasn't found an engineering job
yet, but he's thinking about looking in Kisumu. This
way he will be able to spend more time with Omar.
We can never live like man and wife again after what
has happened. He doesn't trust me and I don't trust
him, but for Omar's sake we try to be courteous to
each other.

Thank you for all your help. I couldn't have
found Omar without you. I owe you my happiness.

And thanks for lending me the money. I'll find a
way of paying you back, I promise.

Your loving sister
Babs'

ॐॐॐ

August 2014

The postman came while Mark and Lavinia were having
breakfast. Lavinia jumped up like a child and rushed to
the front door.

'There might be some more replies to the wedding
invitations,' she explained to Mark, who was buttering
his toast.

She came back clutching a pile of letters and
pamphlets, some of them bills, most of them junk mail,
and amongst them, three cream-coloured envelopes
fringed with gilt.

'This one's from Africa,' she said, handing Mark an envelope with a large colourful stamp on it.

'It's from Babs!' he exclaimed, licking marmalade off his fingers and wiping them on his jeans before tearing it open.

'What does she say?' asked Lavinia.

'She's coming to the wedding!'

Dear Mark,

Of course I'll come to your wedding! I wouldn't miss it for the world! Unfortunately I can't bring Omar, but Sayid said he would look after him for a week. I might put the flat on the market while I'm in England. If I sold it I could pay you back the money I owe you and, if there's anything left over, I might even be able to pay off my bride price!

I love living here. Every day I wake up to blue skies and sunshine. As you know, Kisumu is a large city, but it is so spacious and relaxed it feels like a smaller town. There are a couple of nature reserves nearby. I took Omar to the Wildlife Impala Park on the banks of the lakeside, and he loved it! He can't stop talking about the leopards and peacocks. I hope one day you and Lavinia can come and visit us here.

Good luck with the wedding arrangements. I can't wait to see you in September!

All my love,

Babs

THE PIED RATCATCHER

Señora Diaz looked up from the pile of papers on the desk in front of her, leaned back and rubbed her eyes as well as she could without smudging her mascara. It was getting dark outside. The administrator and the committee members had left several hours ago, but she wanted to go over the details once more before the annual general meeting tomorrow. She chuckled to herself. They would never catch her! The owners were so stupid – they would never notice that she had signed a contract for the maintenance of garden machinery that cost more than the machinery itself! Luckily most of the owners were foreigners who only stayed for a few months each year: the Scandinavians came to escape the dark winter days of the North, and the English to avoid yet another disappointing summer on their native soil. Of course, there were always trouble-makers among those who lived here all the year round. Like that woman Brenda who fed the feral cats. She was always arguing with the gardeners, who complained because the cats dug up the flower beds. Sra. Diaz wanted to eliminate the Cat Feeding Programme as it would save the punters a couple of thousand euros and she would be able to present them with a balanced budget!

While she was contemplating ways of reducing next year's spending, there was a soft tap at the door. It was so gentle that at first she thought she had imagined it. There it was again, slightly louder and more persistent. Who would come to the office so late in the day? Perhaps it was one of the guards, or a committee member who had forgotten something.

Sra. Diaz stood up and glanced in the mirror above the safe, arranging her recently coiffed golden curls around her pretty doll's face.

'Not bad for a grandmother,' she thought to herself.

'Come in,' she called out.

The door opened and an apparition appeared before her. She couldn't prevent herself from gasping. A tall thin man with blonde wavy hair down to his shoulders filled the door frame. His face was weather beaten and wrinkled, his twinkling eyes a piercing blue. His nose was long and hooked, above a smile that curved from ear to ear. It wasn't just his facial features that were unusual. He was wearing a tunic made of red and yellow patches over yellow tights. His red leather shoes were pointed and turned up at the end.

Didn't he know that colour-blocking went out of fashion years ago?

'Good evening, señora,' he said with a theatrical flourish, removing a small red cap from his head and bowing with a sweeping gesture, placing one foot behind the other.

Sra. Diaz was lost for words.

'Allow me to introduce myself!'

He plucked a card from his breast pocket with a long bony forefinger and thumb and presented it to Sra. Diaz, who took it and looked at it carefully. The writing was in a gothic script and difficult to decipher. She read the inscription out loud:

> P. Piper Pets Control
> Rats a Speciality
> Environmentally Friendly
> Mijas, Costa del Sol
> 95 254 7783

'What does that mean – *Environmentally Friendly*?' asked Sra. Diaz, not sure what else to say.

'It means that I can remove any unwanted creatures, for example rats, mice, cockroaches, without using poison. My methods are 100% effective and the results are permanent.'

'And how would you do that?'

He tapped a flute that was tucked under a leather belt at his waist.

'I enchant them with my music.'

'You enchant them!'

'Yes. Just as a snake charmer knows how to mesmerise a dangerous snake. Each animal responds to a different kind of music. It is my skill to know which creature likes what. For example, cockroaches tend to like slow melodic music of a romantic nature. Mice, by contrast, like something a bit lively, and so forth.'

'There's a typo – you've written '*pets*' instead of '*pest*!"

'Ah well, Madam, my services cover all eventualities. For example, I hear you are having a small problem with the cat population?'

'Well, yes I am as a matter of fact ... '

'I could resolve the situation for you within hours.'

'That would be one in the eye for Brenda,' she thought.

Then she recovered herself.

'Look, I am sorry, but this is most irregular ... '

'I took the liberty of drawing up a contract.'

With another sweeping gesture he removed a piece of parchment rolled up and tied with a red ribbon from his hip pocket and handed it to her.

'If you would care to peruse it ... '

Sra. Diaz untied the ribbon and smoothed out the paper that was yellowing and curling up at the corners.

'You will notice that my fee is very reasonable – only €300, which would include a little something for yourself of course. There is a two-year money-back guarantee. You have nothing to lose!'

'Mmmm, well, it does sound interesting and the price is reasonable ... '

'There is only one condition – that I am paid in cash before I carry out the work!'

'Well normally of course we would have to consider other tenders, but the fee is not exorbitant and it would save us money in the long run. I could take it out of petty cash. No-one would be any the wiser ... '

After signing the contract, Sra. Diaz turned around and bent down in front of the safe. She deliberately placed her body between the piper and the combination lock, so that he could not see what she was doing. Before opening the door, she glanced up at the mirror; the rat catcher was busy polishing his flute with a red silk handkerchief that he had produced from yet another pocket. She took out a thin pile of new notes held together with a glued strip of paper, closed the safe door and sat down at the desk again. Slowly she counted out the €50 bills as she peeled them off one by one, looking up at him after placing each one in front of him. When she came to the sixth note, he refused it with a wave of his hand. She took it and slipped it into her pocket.

'Thank you, señor, it is a pleasure doing business with you.'

'Thank you, madam. Rest assured, you will have no more problems in the furry feline department.'

She went to shake hands with him, but with a lavish gesture he bowed and kissed her hand, spun around and left the room on silent feet, closing the door behind him.

Early the next morning, as the sun rose over the mountains and drenched the town with golden light, a quaint figure picked his way down the hillside via the goat track until he reached the paved road at the entrance to the community, where he took out his pipe and started to play. At first the melody was slow and mournful. A few cats living close by were busy eating their breakfast. When they heard the music they lifted their noses from their bowls and listened, captivated. It reminded them of the times when they were kittens, safe and warm under their mother's care. Soon half a dozen cats made their way to where the piper was standing. Within a few minutes he was surrounded by felines from all corners of the community. He turned around towards the mountain and, picking up the pace of the music, led them up the winding path. There were:

> Fat cats, black cats, mongrel cats with twisted tails.
> Lean cats, mean cats, cats who fought with teeth and nails

Black and white with mangy fur
　　and torn ears – no time to purr.
Ginger cats with green eyes glistening
Tabby cats with long ears listening
Fluffy cats as white as snow.
Proud Persians, vain and slow
A Siamese stepped daintily placing her feet,
　　with her tail in the air, in time to the beat.
Two little kittens did their best,
Straining with their short legs to keep up with the
　　rest.

One of the owners spotted the line of cats disappearing up the mountainside.

'Binky! Twinky!' he shouted in desperation, but they did not turn a whisker. He stood watching helplessly as the piper came to a cave in the hillside. One by one the cats followed him into the gaping hollow. Then the music stopped and a huge boulder rolled over the entrance to the cave, the noise echoing through the valley below. The two kittens, arriving at the last minute, managed to find a small crack and squeezed their tiny bodies through it to disappear with the rest.

☙◦۞◦❧

For a couple of weeks a strange stillness descended upon the community. Some of the pet owners had climbed the mountain in search of the cave, but could find no trace of it. The gardeners hoed the flower beds in peace. The President balanced the budget and was re-elected.

Then one morning an owner came into the office to complain about seeing a rat on his terrace. Sra. Diaz called out to one of the gardeners:

'José! Do we have any of the rat poison left? Can you put some down at No. 49?'

But the problem didn't stop there. Each day more and more people came to lodge their complaints. In the end, the President had to lock herself in the office while angry owners banged on the door and shouted through the windows. A guard had to be posted outside to keep them at bay.

There were rats everywhere.

You could hear them scuffling and squeaking as they rummaged in the rubbish. Long-tailed rats with beady eyes slithered along the gutters. Rats with fat bellies hid under the tables in the restaurant, feeding on the crumbs and frightening away the customers. They would brush against women's legs or run over their sandaled feet with scratchy claws until the diners ran out screaming.

Sra. Diaz called the head gardener into the office.

'You have to do something to get rid of the rats. Can't you put down more poison?'

'I have, señora, but the rats seem to thrive on it. They eat the poisoned food, but instead of dying, they put on weight!'

❧⋙⋘❧

That evening, after a long day in the office scrutinizing the books, Sra. Diaz came home. She thought she would lie down and rest for a few minutes. Going into the bedroom in the half-light, she heard a strange scuffling sound followed by a squeak. She switched on the light and let out a scream. A white rat with red-rimmed eyes was sitting in the corner, staring at her, its whiskers twitching. Sra. Diaz turned and ran out, slamming the bedroom door behind her.

Her hand trembling and her heart pounding, she picked up the phone.

'Quick! Quick! Come *pronto*! There's an emergency!'

The guard couldn't quite understand what the problem was, but within five minutes he was ringing her doorbell. Sra. Diaz opened the door looking dishevelled and wild-eyed.

'Alfonso! Thank goodness you've come!'

With one hand on her chest, she pointed towards the closed bedroom door.

'There's a horrible rat in there.'

The guard opened the door gingerly, not quite sure how he would catch the rodent if he found it. He searched all around the bedroom, moving the curtains aside with his torch, but could find nothing.

'In the morning I'll bring you some mouse traps,' he offered.

'But what shall I do tonight?'

'Perhaps you should sleep in the living room.'

After Alfonso had left, Sra. Diaz dragged some blankets out of the cupboard and curled up on the couch, where she spent a restless night, starting every time she heard a creaking noise.

❧◈☙

The next morning, her hair once more arranged in elegant waves but her face pale under her makeup, Sra. Diaz appeared in the office.

'Mary, get me that man on the phone!' she ordered the secretary.

'What man?' replied Mary in bewilderment.

Sra. Diaz rummaged in her handbag and took out a card, throwing it across the desk at her. Mary dialled the number and waited.

'There's no answer – oh wait a minute! The line has been disconnected!'

'What am I to do? Will no one rid me of these pestilent beasts?'

Sra. Diaz called in one of the guards.

'Fernando, go to this village on you motor bike and see if you can find this man and bring him here. Tell him I need his services. It's in the mountains somewhere, not very far from here.'

The guard left, squinting at the strange writing on the card.

Two hours later he returned. He was on his own.

'I found the village and I went to the house, but it was in ruins. I asked an old lady if she knew the man who lived there. She said that she remembered him, but he had left 20 years ago, and she had neither seen nor heard of him since.'

So the community became overrun by a plague of rats. Many of the owners abandoned their villas and returned to the countries from whence they had come. Some moved to other villages.

And so the community became a ghost town. Without the gardeners to tend them, the gardens became overgrown. The paint peeled off the houses and they started to crumble and fall into disrepair. Only the rats flourished as they swarmed over the empty buildings.

But on a balmy summer's night, when the moon shines full on the sea, some say you can still hear the faint sound of a flute wafting down the mountains on a gentle breeze.

So listen all you people who don't like cats
You may end up with a plague of rats!

THE MAN WHO COULD
SLOW DOWN TIME

Steve sat on a boulder, screened by a bush. Perspiration dripped down his bronzed face. He watched the ibex with its magnificent pair of curved horns as it ascended the craggy slope of the mountain. When it reached the rock, it stopped, just as he had hoped, and surveyed the surrounding landscape, turning its proud head. It was silhouetted against a deep blue sky with a bright white cloud just behind it. He raised his camera and pressed the button.

'Got it!' he exclaimed to himself.

He looked at the photo in the viewer. It was a perfect shot.

He loved taking pictures of wild animals, but they were the most difficult to capture on camera. Just when you had them lined up in the frame, they would move! He practised on his cat at home, but even Felix would sense when his master wanted him to sit still and would deliberately stretch and yawn or jump off the chair. Still, Steve had achieved a small measure of success as an amateur photographer, and had even had an exhibition at the cultural centre in town.

He took a swig of brandy from his hip flask and looked out over the panorama of the Mediterranean. In the summer heat, the sky seemed to melt into the sea. A small fishing village with its white-washed houses and terracotta roofs clung to the coastline. To his right, the rugged hills descended into a blue-green expanse of water. He breathed in the warm smell of the baked earth and wild herbs. Life was good!

It was time to head home before the midday heat made walking in the sun unbearable. He put his camera in his back-pack and climbed down the goats' path, being careful not to slip on the shale.

Half an hour later he reached the *cortijo* on the outskirts of town. He stepped into its cool shade with a sense of relief. After cooking himself some fish and *patatas a la pobre* in the farmhouse kitchen, he sat down to his lunch out on the terrace, which was shaded by overhanging grape vines.

When he had finished his meal, he left the dirty dishes in the sink and lay down on his bed for his afternoon siesta. He was feeling exhausted after the early start and then the climb up the mountain. He had expected to fall into a dead sleep, but instead he lay there, contemplating the contrast between the white wall beyond the French windows, the yellow sunshade and the blue sky.

His thoughts drifted back to his time in London, commuting to work on the Tube, wrestling with the intricacies of tax law in a basement office. Everything was grey. The blinds were grey, the carpet was grey, the sky was grey. He would emerge at 5.30 p.m., only to make his way home in the rain. Now he was retired and living the dream. He had definitely made the right decision to sell his house in the suburbs of London and move here.

The only problem was that time passed too quickly. He had chosen to live in what he had thought was a sleepy Spanish village, but there was always something going on. The local people loved fiestas and would often dance and sing until the early hours of the morning. He also attended Spanish classes in a charming little building with wooden beams, built around a central courtyard with a fountain that played in the breeze. To tell the truth, he hadn't made much progress, but he had enjoyed meeting the other students, most of whom were women. Some of them flirted with him, but he wasn't quite ready for a relationship yet. He still hadn't recovered from his wife's passing, four years ago. They had been childhood sweethearts so he had never been on a proper date. He had heard of speed dating, but didn't think he would be any good at it.

He had taken up photography because it was something he had always wanted to do. Sometimes English people came out here thinking it would be like an extended holiday, only to find that, after a couple of weeks, they were bored stiff, and would end up spending their days playing bridge or drinking gin and tonic on the terrace. He didn't want to fall into either trap.

But now that he had finally found paradise, how could he stop the relentless march of time? He wanted to reach out and grasp the moment and hold onto it, but the bright hot days and balmy nights slipped through his fingers. He remembered a poem that someone had read out in Assembly many years ago when he was a schoolboy about how time crawled when you were young, then it ran as you grew older. How could he slow time down? Of course, time was relative. It was the same for everyone, whether you were old or young.

But it was the perception of time that was different. It had certainly gone slowly when he was at school, especially during Latin classes. He could never see the point of learning a dead language. Perhaps if he had paid more attention, he would find Spanish easier to learn. When he was sitting in his office, yearning for fresh air and green fields, time had crept. And now, because he was enjoying himself, time zoomed by so fast he felt he couldn't keep up with it.

He looked at his watch. It was 4 p.m. He hadn't been able to sleep, but felt revived from having rested in the coolness of his bedroom. He got out of bed and made his way across the hall into the unevenly tiled kitchen with the sloping roof, where he started washing the dishes. Now and again he would glance up from the sink at the crooked rows of olive trees that grew outside the window.

When he had finished, he went into the living room and turned on the television. There was a football match between England and Germany that he wanted to watch. The remote control didn't seem to be working properly. He pressed the button and nothing happened. Then in frustration he banged it on the coffee table. That did the trick. The match had only just begun but it was in slow motion.

'It must be an action replay,' he thought.

He sat, mesmerized by the movements of the players. They were so graceful. Sometimes their actions seemed to defy the laws of gravity. One player was almost horizontal to the ground as he kicked the ball with his right foot towards a teammate on his left. The whole performance was like a ballet with men dressed in shorts. Then someone got control of the ball and kicked it towards the goal. It soared high up in the air in an enormous curve. Steve sat with his mouth open until the ball glanced off the top of the goal post. He let out a grunt of frustration. The action replay had gone on for long enough, so he switched to another channel that was also broadcasting the game. But that was in slow motion too. What was going on here? Had some idiot forgotten to change the camera back to normal speed? He sat and watched the game for another 10 minutes, but he found it tedious at slow speed. When the commercial break came, he was glad to jump up and put the kettle on. But the water took ages to boil. What was happening? After the break he sat down again with his cup of tea. The match was still in slow motion. He tried a different channel. One of those endless detective stories was on, but that was also slowed down, so that their speech was slurred. He watched in fascination for a few minutes, but soon got bored and switched back to the football. Perhaps there was something wrong with the remote control. He would take it in tomorrow and get it repaired or exchanged.

Felix came in through the open doors. He walked along stealthily as if he were stalking prey. When he jumped onto the chair, he moved in a slow arc. Even the cat was affected! Steve ran for his camera in the hope of getting an action shot, but by the time he got back, the cat was curled up on the cushion with one eye closed.

That night he tossed and turned in bed, thinking over the day's events. He remembered something his mother had told him many years ago.

'Be careful what you wish for!'

The next morning he jumped into his mud-spattered jeep to go into town. He noticed that all the other cars were crawling along at a snail's pace. What was wrong with them? Steve put his foot down on the accelerator and wove in and out. A couple of drivers hooted at him. Motorists didn't usually honk their horns in Andalusia unless they saw a friend. He squinted at their faces through the windscreen, but didn't recognize any of them. Then he looked at the speedometer. He was breaking the speed limit! He slowed down to the pace of the other drivers. Just as he reached the traffic lights, they turned red. A pregnant woman crossed in front of him with a baby in a pushchair and two other small children dancing around her. He sat and waited for the lights to change. He waited and waited. An elderly couple crossed from the other direction, looking at him fearfully as if they sensed his impatience and were afraid he was going to start the jeep before they reached the safety of the far pavement. The lights remained red. Perhaps they were broken. Just as he was about to release the handbrake and jump the lights, they turned green.

He found a place to park and walked towards the TV repair shop. The people of Andalusia did not rush at the best of times. Now they were creeping along the pavements or blocking his path by standing in groups to chat to each other.

When he entered the repair shop, there was only one person in front of him, but Steve knew he was in for a long wait. He had lived on the Costa del Sol long enough to know that the local people put socializing before business, and did not appreciate being interrupted by impatient foreigners. So he did what he usually did in similar situations. He adopted the smile of a benevolent simpleton and stood looking around at the items in the shop with interest. When they laughed, he laughed. They were talking so slowly that he could actually understand every word they were saying. While he was waiting, he scrutinized the dusty old TV sets stacked on shelves, waiting to be repaired. When he had finished, he read all the notices and posters on the walls with rapt attention. Finally he turned and watched the passers-by walk along the street. Not once did he drum his fingers on the counter, sigh or betray any sign of impatience or aggravation. After the pair had finished discussing the weather, football, the declining economy, politics and women, the other customer took his leave.

The repair man put both hands on the counter and leaned forward, looking at him over his round wire-rimmed glasses. '*Buenos dias, señor.* What can I do for you?'

Steve showed him the remote control and said it wasn't working properly. First the man tested the batteries. Then he switched on one of the old television sets and pointed the remote control towards it. With a click, a sports programme came on. He surfed through the channels.

'There's nothing wrong with it,' declared the repair man.

'But all the programmes are in slow motion!'

The man looked at the screen and then turned to him with a pitying look. His gaze made Steve feel hot and uncomfortable.

'Well, thanks anyway,' Steve replied, putting the remote control back in his pocket and heading out of the shop.

The next stop was the supermarket. He had to wait longer than usual in the queue at the cashier's desk, but no-one else seemed unduly worried. One old woman emptied her purse and stood there counting out the change. He wanted to scream.

As he drove home, he looked at his watch. It was only 12.15 p.m. It had seemed like a long morning.

When he got home, he had his lunch and tried out the remote control again. The channels were still in slow motion.

'Damn it!' he shouted in frustration, and slammed the remote on the coffee table. Wayne Rooney, who had been dancing across the field like a ballerina, suddenly leapt into action.

'That's more like it!' he exclaimed, and settled down with a bottle of beer to watch the highlights of yesterday's match.

THE TEMPLE OF
THE SLEEPING DRAGON

Jen Shi awoke to the sound of a gong that reverberated throughout the dormitory. Reluctantly he opened his eyes, but all he could see was blackness.

Someone lit a lantern to reveal dozens of sleepy boys pulling themselves up from mattresses that formed several rows upon the flagstones.

He rolled over on his lumpy straw pallet and pulled the blanket over his head.

'Come on, Jen Shi, get up! You'll be late!'

His friend, Chu Lin, was pulling off the cover. Jen Shi rolled onto the cold stone floor, stood up and followed him to the 'sheep dip,' a long narrow pool with steps leading down into it at both ends. It was walled in at either side, so there was no escape. The other boys were lining up to take the plunge one by one. When his turn came, he looked down into the green water. Now and again it was emptied out and cleaned with disinfectant, but this morning the floor looked slimy. As he hesitated, shivering at the top of the stairs, the crush of boys pushed him forward. He stepped down into the icy water, holding onto the side so that he did not slip. The cold shock took his breath away. As the water reached the middle of his chest, he plunged in and swam with a couple of strokes to the end. Then he dipped his head under the water, emerged and scrambled up the steps. He knew that if he came out with dry hair, the teacher would send him back in again. Master Chan sat at the top of the steps, handing out a clean scratchy towel to each boy as he emerged. Jen Shi bowed and thanked him, his teeth chattering. He wrapped the small towel around himself, still shivering from the early morning chill.

After pulling on the clothes that lay folded beside his mattress, Jen Shi followed the other boys across the courtyard. As they reached the narrow upward path to the temple, they fell into single file. Nobody spoke in the hush before daybreak. The only sound to be heard was the soft crunch of cloth shoes on gravel. A new moon hung suspended in the clear sky as Venus rose above the mountains. He could smell the heady scent of incense in the night air.

The temple was guarded by two gilt dragons that gleamed in the light of flaming torches on either side of the massive red doors. At the top of the steep flight of steps he stopped to remove his shoes before entering. He joined a row of students sitting cross-legged before a giant golden statue of Buddha. The cold, hard tiles sent a chill up his spine.

The cavernous temple was built into the mountain, and the rock wall made a natural shrine for the icons. These were lit by oil lamps placed on pieces of stone that jutted out to form shelves. A red banner with gold calligraphy hung above the statue. It read, 'Look within.' Jen Shi contemplated the scenes from the life of Siddhartha that were painted upon a row of red wooden pillars and upon the rock that formed the sloping east wall.

Master Chan entered the temple carrying a stick under his arm. Everyone sat up straight. He was a tall, gaunt man, his posture slightly stooped like a stork. His plain black robe, tied by a girdle at the waist, served to enhance the impression of severity. With a nod of the head, he signalled to the monk, who struck the gong. The first 'Om' reverberated through the temple, followed by the second before the echoes of the first could die away, and then a third. The chanting had begun.

The repetition of the mantras was mesmerizing. It had a soothing effect upon Jen Shi, who would dearly have loved to have fallen back to sleep.

The master walked between the rows with his stick, poking any boy who slumped forward.

By the time they came out of the temple, the sky was growing light, throwing the Mountain of the Sleeping Dragon into silhouette. A cock crowed in the distance.

They made their way over to a long stone building that served as an exercise room. Two china urns stood at either side of the entrance. The perfume of floral incense that rose from them failed to mask the odour of stale perspiration, just as the pale morning sun, slanting in from the open windows, failed to warm the flagstones. Rows of wooden tables, worn and splintered, stretched the length of the room.

Jen Shi could hear clatter from the kitchen next door. The smell of food cooking made his stomach rumble.

Master Chan situated himself at one end of the room. With one strike of his stick, all the boys jumped onto a low table. At the second strike, they jumped down onto the floor again. Altogether they must have jumped onto the tables a hundred times. Jen Shi felt his thigh muscles aching, but did not dare to take a rest.

The master's stick came down relentlessly. Sweat dripped down his face and into his eyes. Just when Jen Shi thought he could go on no longer, the master stopped. All the students bowed to the teacher and filed out to the refectory.

He stood in line behind Chu Lin, holding his bowl.

'What's for breakfast?' asked Jen Shi.

'I think it's rice gruel,' replied his friend.

This was their little joke. It was always rice gruel.

After breakfast they walked over to a wooden building, formerly used as a barn, that was now divided into several classrooms. Anatomy was their first lesson of the day. The boys filed in and sat on the floor in a semi-circle.

The walls were covered in charts and diagrams, many of them curling up at the bottom. One or two of the pictures of the human body had gratuitous comments added by a student with an active imagination.

A short man with a bald head stood at the front of the class dressed in a high-necked yellow jacket fastened with white toggles. Master Feng always had a fat smile on his oily face and spoke with a high-pitched voice, but no-one made fun of him.

The teacher pointed to a chart demonstrating the vital energy centres or *chakras* in the body.

'How many *chakras* are there in the human body?' he asked, pointing at one of the boys with his stick.

The boy stood up.

'108, sir.'

'Correct, Mi Shu. Sit down.'

He paced backwards and forwards, tapping the cane against the palm of his hand.

'How many of the points are fatal ... Jen Shi?'

Jen Shi sprang to his feet. Perspiration prickled his temples. He looked over to Chu Lin, who was casually doodling something in his notebook. How could his friend be so indifferent to his suffering? Then he recognized a number amidst the scribble.

'36, sir!'

'Correct!' replied Master Jung. 'It is important to remember that the *chakras* can be used both to kill or heal, depending upon the pressure applied to them. If you use acupuncture or massage, you can heal your patient. If you strike him sharply on certain points, you can kill him.'

The students whispered and shifted in their seats.

'However, I shall not be showing you the 36 fatal points today.'

A disappointed murmur rose from the group.

'This information is secret, and will only be revealed to a few trusted senior students. For your homework,' the master continued, 'you must memorize the head *chakras*. Copy them down in your books. There will be a test.'

The students groaned.

'Silence!' he snapped. The grumbling ceased abruptly.

The boys sat on the floor making swift strokes with their brushes. Some calligraphy was more graceful than others. Jen Shi accidentally dropped a blot of ink on his notebook.

After class, Jen Shi and Chu Lin walked over to the temple to collect the wooden pails. It was their task today to sweep and mop the temple floor, but first they had to bring the water. They raced down the mountainside with the empty buckets swinging from hand-carved yokes, trying not to slip in the dirt or trip on the larger stones. With the advantage of his long legs, Jen Shi was the first to arrive at the river's edge. The two boys filled their pails at the rushing stream, but one of Jen Shi's buckets had a leak in it, so he had to line it with large flat leaves. Chu Lin crouched on a boulder, attempting to catch a fish with his hands. Using the rocks as stepping stones, Jen Shi stole up behind him and tried to push him into the icy water, but Chu Lin was too fast for him. He leapt up like a frog and jumped to another stone. In this way Jen Shi chased him, laughing, to the river bank.

They put the yokes across their young shoulders and balanced a bucket at each end. The ascent was not so easy, and Jen Shi had to stop and put down his burden under the pretence of admiring the scenery. A golden eagle hovered and swooped in the valley below him. Above, the sun rose over the mountain peaks that gave the name of 'Sleeping Dragon' to the temple built into its precipitous slopes. The sky overhead was a clear blue, but the clouds were amassing behind the mountain range. There would be rain later in the day.

'Hurry up, Jen Shi,' called Chu Lin. 'All the water will drain out of your bucket!'

Jen Shi picked up the yoke and caught up with him, trying to ignore the burning sensation in his calves.

By the time they arrived at the temple, his leaky bucket was half empty. He ran round to the little room at the back and pulled out another pail into which he poured what was left of the water. Then he picked up two brooms made of twigs bound together with twine, and they started at opposite ends to sweep the floor, making their way towards the middle. The object of the game was to be the first to finish his half. Jen Shi found the swishing sound of the broom soothing as he brushed it rhythmically against the stone floor. Chu Lin beat him to the central line. Jen Shi was in bad form today.

They returned the brooms to the small room and brought out the mops. A monk,who was pouring oil into the lamps on the altar, turned round at the sound of their whispering. After that, they did their best to suppress their laughter as they carried out a mopping race. Master Chu came in and struck the gong.

Now it was time for their first martial arts class of the day. They hurried to the courtyard, which was comprised of a raised paved dais, lined with benches on two sides where spectators could sit. At one end a broad flight of steps led up to red double doors. Inside was a large room where weapons and other equipment were stored, and where the students trained on rainy days.

Most of the other students were already lined up, standing 'at ease' with their legs apart and their hands behind their backs.

Master Jung stood before them with his broad shoulders held back, a slim, muscular man of average height. He looked about 30, but several strands of grey in his black shaggy hair indicated that he might be older than he appeared. He wore an immaculate white cotton tunic over a pair of loose-fitting black trousers, tied with a white belt. He had a stillness about him that commanded authority.

'You are fortunate to be students at one of the best martial arts temples in the country!' the teacher announced.

Jen Shi wondered what the other schools were like.

First they did some stretching exercises. Then they stood in lines and practised punches and kicks to the master's count.

'White Crane spreads his wings!' called Master Jung.

All the students lifted their left leg, bent at the knee. At the same time, they raised their arms, curved at the wrists, their fingers splayed out like the wing feathers of a bird. They held the position.

The multi-coloured flags flapped from the red poles that lined the courtyard, and in the distance, Jen Shi could hear the whir of prayer wheels.

'Jen Shi, bend your leg!'

He lowered his stance, and in doing so, wobbled. With an effort of will, he regained his balance.

The sun was now almost overhead, beating down on him relentlessly. The sweat trickled from his forehead and down his torso. A fly landed on his nose. He tried to blow it away but it kept coming back.

'Steady!' commanded Master Jung in a threatening tone. He walked amongst the students, adjusting their stances.

Jen Shi didn't know how much longer he could maintain the position, but no-one dared move without the master's orders.

'White Crane stands on two legs!'

With a sigh of relief, the boys lowered their left foot to the ground.

'Don't collapse!'

They all stood to attention.

Then they did the same thing again, only this time raising their right leg.

By the time they had finished, Jen Shi's legs were shaking with the stress on his muscles.

'Form One!' shouted the master.

The younger students lined up, and, at the teacher's count, executed a series of punches, kicks, jumps and turns, choreographed into what looked like one flowing dance. At the end they bowed to the other students and the master, who announced the next form.

The middle pupils, including Jen Shi, stepped forward and performed in front of the rest of the group. All the movements were to be done simultaneously, so if anyone made a mistake, it became painfully obvious. Jen Shi managed to keep up with the others and joined them in a bow when they had finished.

Then the seven advanced students came to the centre of the courtyard. Their movements were complex, liquid and lightening fast, like flames. Their baggy pants and loose jackets snapped as they executed the moves. When they took their bow, all the younger boys applauded.

Next the students were paired off to practice sparring. The master called out Jen Shi and Mi Shu. They bowed to each other and the contest began. They knew they were supposed to pull their punches as any full-force strike could cause injury or even death. Mi Shu was an aggressive fighter. At first, Jen Shi responded to his attacks by blocking and counter-striking in one move. Sometimes Mi Shu would fake right and strike left. Jen Shu tried to stay calm, focusing on his opponent's movements. Then he saw his opportunity, and, raising his right leg, he kicked to Mi Shu's chin. Mi Shu avoided the kick by stepping to one side, turning his body. At the same time he caught Jen Shi by the ankle and tipped him over backwards. Everyone laughed.

Jen Shi sprang up from the ground and dusted himself down, feeling mortified.

'Jen Shi, you are showing off with your long legs and fancy high kicks again!' reprimanded the master.

'What are the weaknesses of this attack?' he asked, addressing the other students.

'His balance is poor when standing on one leg!'

'He has left his lower body unprotected and has thus exposed it to attack!'

'A high kick takes too long and he telegraphs his intention to his opponent, giving him time to avoid it!'

'Good! O.K., Jen Shi, go back to your place.'

Feeling shame-faced, Jen Shi shambled back to the row of boys, where he took his place next to Chu Lin.

'Don't worry,' whispered Chu Lin, patting him on the shoulder.

Jen Shi was glad when the bell for lunch sounded.

'What's on the menu today?' asked Chu Lin.

'Oh, I think it's rice and vegetables.'

Lunch usually consisted of rice and whatever vegetables were available from the temple's kitchen garden. Sometimes there were a few nuts thrown in. Today some eggs had been scrambled into the mixture. Jen Shi was hungry, and cleaned out his bowl in no time. There never seemed to be quite enough food to satisfy his appetite.

As they left the canteen, an excited whisper circulated amongst the boys.

'The post is here!'

They made their way over to a small enclosed courtyard next to the refectory, where one of the senior boys was standing with a handful of letters and a parcel. The walls were so high that it was impossible for the teachers to spy on them. As he announced the name on each letter, a boy came forward and took his mail. In the end, only the coveted parcel remained. The senior student scrutinized the lettering. 'Soo Ying,' he called out. Some of the other boys crowded around the lucky student, curious to see what the package contained.

As they walked away empty-handed, Chu Lin noticed tears in his friend's eyes.

'What's the matter, Jen Shi?' he asked.

'I didn't get anything from my parents,' he mumbled, looking at the ground as he walked.

'But you never get anything from your parents!' Chu Lin commented.

'Today is my 16th birthday! They forgot!'

Chu Lin felt sad for him, but didn't know what to do.

'Never mind. Come on, we have to do our homework for tomorrow.'

They found a grassy patch in the apple orchard, where they tested each other on head *chakras*.

A bell tinkled above the sound of bird song.

'What's the next class?' asked Jen Shi, gathering up his books.

'Herbal Medicine.'

They set off for the classroom, where they joined the other boys sitting in a circle on the rough wooden floor. The room was a mirror image of the Anatomy class except that the walls were furnished with scrolls and diagrams of plants.

Master Tang appeared, tall and thin with beady eyes, swishing his bamboo stick. His lank hair was tied back in a pony tail. He reminded Jen Shi of a vulture.

'Today we are going to study ginkgo. What can you tell me about it, Fu Shen?'

'It's the oldest tree in the world, sir.'

'Correct! According to the legendary emperor and sage, Shen Nung, it is good for the heart and lungs. It can also be used to treat asthma and chilblains, and may help to improve the memory.'

Master Tang fixed his glinting eyes on one of the students in the front row.

'Some of you boys may find it useful.'

He indicated a picture of the fan-shaped leaves.

'There is both a male and female tree.'

The boys giggled.

Thwackkk! The master cracked his cane on the desk.

'The female tree produces orange-yellow fruit. We are going to find a tree, and I want you to bring back specimens of both the leaves and the fruit.'

The students left their notebooks on the floor and went outside. The storm clouds that had been gathering since that morning were now almost black overhead. There was a crack of thunder and the rain poured down.

The master strode ahead of them, swinging his cane.

'Come on boys! Rain is a blessing of nature.'

By the time they had reached the edge of the forest, they were all soaked to the skin. It was hard to walk along the muddy path and climb the boulders without slipping. Although the trees formed a natural panoply that sheltered them from the rain, the water continued to patter on the leaves and trickle down the trunks.

Master Tang stopped in front of a tree that towered 50 feet above them.

'This is the mighty ginkgo! Collect your samples!'

Most of the leaves and apricot-size fruit were above their grasp, so a couple of youngsters shinned up the tree and showered down specimens to the pupils standing below. The boys ran around, competing with each other to catch the leaves and berries before they hit the ground.

As the students left the shelter of the woods, the rain came down in torrents. Jen Shi looked up at the mountain range. For a split second, a flash of lightening threw the silhouette of the dragon's back into relief. Then the dragon's roar shook the ground under their feet.

'The dragon is angry,' thought Jen Shi.

Back in the classroom, they took their leaves and fruit from their drenched bags and started to draw them in their notebooks. When the master turned his back, Mei Ling threw a piece of fruit at another boy's head, hitting his target with precision.

'Aaaiiii!' shouted the boy.

Master Tang wheeled round.

'Who made that noise?' he asked.

Ming Yip stood up, rubbing his head.

'Someone threw something at me!'

'Who was it?' the teacher asked, glaring at the boys and pacing backwards and forwards.

Nobody answered.

'If no-one will confess, I shall have to punish you all!'

'It was Mei Ling!' called out a thin weasly boy.

'Very good, Mei Ling. You must do 20 push-ups after class. And you, Chen Fu, can do 30 for telling tales!'

Everybody laughed except for the two boys in question.

'Class dismissed!'

The pupils filed out the door, only to gather outside the window in the rain to jeer at the culprits as they took their punishment.

The friends splashed through the mud as they ran across to the kitchen. A sudden flash of lightening lit up the dark storm clouds.

The kitchen was a long, low hut adjoining the refectory.

Inside it was warm and cosy. At the far end of the room, steam rose from a large soot-blackened cauldron that hung from a tripod over an open fire. Even though it was still early, the lanterns had already been lit.

Rain thudded against the window panes to his left. A loose shutter rattled in the gusty wind.

On the opposite wall, crockery was stacked on a wooden board, and on the shelf above it, giant cooking pots and pans were stored. Ladles and other large utensils hung from hooks attached to low beams.

A faint high-pitched squeak reached Jen Shi's ears. Looking down to the right, he noticed rice seeping from small holes in bulging sacks piled up in the corner. Mice darted in and out leaving a trail of tiny flour footprints as they dodged the scurrying feet of the kitchen workers. A fat black and white cat glared down at the rodent invaders from the top of a cupboard.

Jen Shi liked kitchen duty. Sometimes they could filch an extra mouthful of food when no-one was looking. Their clothes soon began to dry out from the heat of the wood-fueled oven.

The baker, a stocky man with bulging muscles, was bending over one of several large trestle tables in the centre of the room making sticky buns stuffed with a sweet coconut mixture. The smell of baking rolls made Jen Shi's mouth water.

Chu Lin was assigned dish-washing duty, which entailed standing at a sink and scrubbing pots and pans in luke-warm dirty water. It was a thankless task. He piled them up on the wooden draining board, but even after he had washed them, the dents were still ingrained with dirt and grease.

Jen Shi helped to prepare the evening meal – flat noodles and whatever vegetables were left over from lunch. He enjoyed kneading the dough and rolling it out on the floured table. When the pasta was flat and even, the chef came over, and with swift movements of a sharp knife, he cut it into long thin parallel strips without pausing between slices.

'That's how it's done!' he remarked with a sneer of pride.

Jen Shi wondered what the chef might have done to a dangerous attacker.

The storm had blown over by the time they had finished. A few last drops of water dripped from the roof tiles into muddy puddles that reflected the grey cloudy sky. The two boys headed off to the courtyard for their next martial arts practice. Chu Lin stopped in a doorway. After checking that no-one else was around, he pulled out a bun from a secret pocket that he had sewn inside his trousers.

'Happy birthday!' he grinned, offering it to his friend.

Jen Shi couldn't believe his luck or the generosity of his friend. Although he could have swallowed the bun in a couple of bites, he broke it in half and gave part of it back to Chu Lin, who refused to accept it at first. However, the mouth-watering smell of yeast and coconut mixed with honey was too enticing for him to resist. They both stood in the doorway devouring their stolen goods. Steam rose from the filling, which was still hot. Even so, that did not prevent them from finishing the bun quickly.

'*Shr shr!*' Jen Shi said, wiping the crumbs from his face. 'Thank you!'

The Kung Fu class was grueling and lasted another two hours. At last the gong sounded, and the boys would gladly have gone for dinner. The bun had only whetted their appetite. But first they had to go to meditation.

The students filed into the temple and sat down on the stone floor.

A monk had lit the incense and was waving a censor in front of the giant golden Buddha.

Jen Shi looked at the statue before him that mirrored his position. The Buddha's eyes were half-closed and a serene expression pervaded his gently smiling face.

'What does the compassionate Buddha care for me?' he thought. 'All day every day I am tired and hungry. I have to suffer the heat of the sun and the cold of the wind and water. Then today my mother and father forgot my birthday!'

A wizened old man with white hair and a long wispy beard entered the temple. All the boys sat up straight. He leaned on his stick as he walked. The Grandmaster sat down stiffly on a wooden throne-like chair placed by the entrance, adjusting his jade green embroidered tunic over his white trousers. He rested his gnarled hands on his gnarled cane and surveyed the students. Despite his advanced years, his eyes were bright and piercing. He nodded to the monk, who struck the gong, and the boys closed their eyes.

The evening meditation had begun.

Jen Shi was hopeless at meditation. He was exhausted from his daily routine and just wanted to sleep. His joints and muscles ached, but instead he had to sit with a straight back on the hard floor for an hour without fidgeting, which made concentration difficult.

He tried to empty his mind, only to find that it jumped around all over the place like a mad monkey. No sooner had he managed to put one thought aside, when another one popped up. He knew that the trick was to find the space between two thoughts, but how could he?

He thought of the students laughing at him when he was toppled by Mi Shu. There he went again, letting his mind wander. It was always the same. He emptied it out and started again. He thought of the delicious bun still warm from the oven. He made his mind a blank parchment and tried again. Then he thought of the test tomorrow. He couldn't remember the head *chakras*! This was a total waste of time.

Wait a minute! What was that? For a moment he glimpsed a gap between his thoughts. He squeezed through it and found himself looking down at the earth and all the other planets. Shooting stars whizzed past like exploding fireworks. He felt himself zoom backwards until he could see the entire solar system. The planets were not arranged neatly in a straight line, the way he had seen them on a scroll in the library. They were all over the place, each following its own path.

There was bright Venus, the colour of sandstone, swathed in sulphurous clouds, and Mercury, closer to the sun, pitted with craters like an adolescent's skin.

By contrast, Earth shone emerald green and sapphire blue like a precious jewel, gilded with sandy deserts, wrapped in wispy white clouds.

Next he approached the barren surface of Mars, with its dunes, river valleys and canyons. The red dust and sand made it glow like an orange-red marble.

Sailing on solar winds, he came to the giant planets – first majestic Jupiter loomed before him, its gossamer dust rings shining like a halo. The surface was striped with a frieze of blue and peach bands in constant motion. As he drew nearer, he could see that it was tormented by electric storms as bolts of lightening blazed up white and sizzling.

He swooped around it past a sprinkling of moons. Europa, the ice queen, glided serenely by, her smooth white face concealing secret lakes beneath the surface.

In contrast, her sister, Io, seethed with volcanic eruptions, spumes of molten lava turning to frozen sulphur, lending her a yellow complexion.

From there he journeyed on to Saturn, flattened at each pole like a padre's hat. He skated around her icy rings, breathtaking in colour like a girl's striped skirt. He brushed past Titan, one of her moons, which was as green as an apple growing in the orchard, rimmed with lemon yellow.

Jen Shi swept past her other moons and moonlets and on to pale blue Uranus, its rings almost at right angles to the sun, as if it was tipped sideways like a drunken monk. The concentric circles made him think of a target board that he had used in archery.

Jen Shi's journey took him on to Neptune, the icy blue giant, with its eight moons. As he came closer to the surface, he noticed geysers spouting gaseous vapour.

Speeding on into the void, he looked back at distant Neptune, which now appeared like an azure bead on a dark blue velvet cloth, scattered with diamond chips.

Ooops! He just missed a black hole!

After several eons he came to Pluto, the dwarf planet, pink-beige in the pale light emitted by the distant sun, and even smaller than the earth's moon. He had now arrived at the far reaches of the solar system.

A myriad pinpricks of light sparkled in the sky, some larger and brighter than others. He drew back again and the sun became just one of a billion stars in the Milky Way. As he flew on faster than the speed of light, the Milky Way became one of a trillion galaxies. Between each galaxy were vast expanses of empty space. He must be at the edge of the universe by now. But when he turned around he realized that the stream of galaxies formed an infinity symbol resembling a figure of eight and that he was at the centre!

The whole universe was displayed before him. Jen Shi could hear a humming sound like music. He was in ecstasy, full of love and peace. He was one with the Universe.

Someone was shaking his shoulder. He opened his eyes to see everyone else standing before the Grandmaster. Jen Shi struggled to his feet and bowed with the rest.

'Class dismissed!' The boys turned and shuffled out. Just as Jen Shi was about to follow them, the master called out his name.

'Jen Shi, stay behind!'

When they were alone, the Grandmaster addressed him.

'Did you not hear the gong? You are not supposed to sleep during meditation!'

'But *Sifu* ...!'

'Enough! Do not answer me back! You need to learn obedience and humility. Do 25 push-ups, and then bring me my tea!'

'*Sifu!*'

Jen Shi bowed, his eyes to the ground and his right hand cupped over his left fist like moss over a stone. Yin and Yang – the soft overcomes the hard. Then he quickly turned away so that the Grandmaster could not see the smile that was spreading over his face.

ACKNOWLEDGEMENTS

I should like to thank all those who helped and encouraged me during the writing of this book, in particular the members of my international 'fan club.'

BIOGRAPHY

Ms. Patterson was born in Cambridge. She grew up in the suburbs of London and went on to study English and Drama at college.

Upon leaving college, she taught English in a secondary school in Surrey.

After moving to London, she found gainful employment working as a guide at Mme. Tussaud's, after which she taught English as a foreign language at a tutorial college.

From 1972–1974 she lived in the South of France, where she studied French and taught English.

Upon her return to England, she taught English at a foreign language school in Oxford. The following year she took a course in Business Studies at Oxford Brookes.

In 1976 she left for New York, where she worked at the Ford Foundation.

In 2013 her first book of short stories entitled *Al Gore goes to Heaven* was published.

Ms. Patterson now lives in Spain, where she continues to write.

OTHER PUBLICATIONS
BY THE SAME AUTHOR:

Al Gore goes to Heaven (short stories)
Becky White (screenplay)